UNDENIABLE

SERENA GREY

Dedication

To my love, who is everything I ever wanted. Here's to a lifetime together, and a love that's undeniable.

Acknowledgments

I'd like to thank all the people who have read, enjoyed, and reviewed my work, as well as all the authors out there who made me fall in love with the art of storytelling.

Thank You Always.

Undeniable

"Protest all you want," he says, "It won't change the fact that this thing we have between us, it's undeniable."

Olivia Wilder fell in love with Jackson Lockewood the first time she laid her eyes on him. She gave him her heart and her love, and ended up alone, heartbroken and with scars that were almost too much for her to bear.

Seven years later, they cross paths again. Jackson is everything she remembers, only more irresistible. Underneath his disdain, his desire to possess her lights a response within her, but she has no desire to rekindle their past, or face the pain of all those years ago.

However, Jackson has no intention of making it easy for her, this time he's determined to make her pay for the past, and for the future they should have had, even if it means destroying her in the process.

Book One

Prologue

Past

"YOU have to get up."

I hear May's voice from what seems like a long way off. That makes no sense, I realize, through the haze of depression in my head. She's sitting right beside my bed.

"Livvie?" I open my eyes at the insistent tone of her voice. She's looking at me, her brow creased in a worried frown. Vaguely, I notice that her back-length curtain of black hair has disappeared, replaced by a short spiky do. When did that happen? When did my best friend change her look? I know the answer. While I was lying in bed feeling too sorry for myself to be a real friend.

The realization makes me all the more miserable, and I indulge the self-pity, feeling the tears that are never far away stinging at the back of my eyelids.

"You can't go on like this," May is saying, "I'm worried about you, Chace is worried about you."

Chace is my roommate. Where is he? He's neither in the room with May, nor hovering by the door looking as helplessly worried as May does now. The last time I saw him, he was picking up the pizza boxes that have littered the floor of my room ever since I started alternating between long periods with no appetite and times when I get so ravenous, I stuff a whole pizza in my mouth so I can feel miserable about it afterwards.

I sigh as the first tear leaks out of my eyes and travels down the side of my face to leave a wet mark on the pillow. Chace deserves a better roommate than someone who can't even get up to clean her own room. May deserves better than a best friend who's been lying in bed for weeks with no intention of ever getting up and facing the world again. They all deserve someone better than me.

May is still looking at me, expecting me to say something. I consider lying. I could tell her that I'm all right, and that she shouldn't worry about me, the sort of things people say when they want you to leave them alone in their misery, but what's the *point? I'm not all right, and anybody can see that.*

"Livvie?"

I ignore her and turn to my other side, away from her, closing my eyes against the light from the window. I keep the curtains drawn to block out the sun and the view, but every small ray of sunlight that finds its way inside adds to the bruised feeling in my heart. The worst thing about being depressed is seeing the sun rise and set every day, and knowing that the world will go on as always, no matter how you're feeling. I bury my face in the pillow. I don't know exactly how long I've been like this, a few weeks, maybe more. It feels like forever. It feels like I've always been in pain, like the pain will never go away.

"Livvie?"

Why won't she leave me alone? Why does she want me to get up when it feels like I'm held down with heavy chains binding all my limbs? I just want to close my eyes and block out the worst of the pain, to try to forget that every moment I'm awake feels like a curse. At least in sleep I can escape the torture. Even if my dreams are painful, they're nothing compared to waking up and realizing that I'm really trapped in the hopelessness that's my life.

"You haven't been showing up to your classes. You've missed deadlines, tests. I know it hurts, but you can't just lie down and hope to die. You have to fight whatever it is you're feeling."

It's easy for her to say. What does she know about pain? I think resentfully. I don't care about school, deadlines, tests, or exams. I don't care about anything.

"What would your parents say if they saw you now?"

Her words conjure my mother's face, her dark hair, and deep green eyes, so like mine. She's smiling, and my dad is with her, laughing happily, his untamable curly blond hair disheveled as always. They look exactly as they always do in my dreams, but when I try to talk to them, they never hear me.

I start to cry, painful, racking sobs that shake my whole body.

May sighs. "I'm sorry Livvie, but I'm not going to let you throw your life away." She lays a soft palm on my shoulder, "You can catch up with your courses if you try. You can get your life back, and it's my job as your friend to make sure you do?"

Good luck. I think silently. Does she think I don't want to get up from this bed? Does she think I wouldn't like to clean my room and make my bed, dress up and even put some make-up on, remember what it's like to be young and happy? It's not that I don't want to get up. It's just that every time I so much as consider it, the black cloud in my head envelopes me, and I just know that nothing is worth it, that nothing is worth getting up again.

"Have you looked at your phone?" She demands softly, "You have thousands of missed calls. I had to lie to Constance and tell her you're fine, and that you just want to be left alone for now. Blythe thinks you're still mad, and you don't want to talk to her."

What about Jackson? I almost ask. But I don't, because I know he's not one of the thousands of missed calls. I know he'll never call. He hates me now, and there's nothing I can do about it.

"I don't know how long you plan on lying here, but I've decided to put a stop to it, and Chace agrees with me." She pauses, as if waiting for me to react, to ask her what her plan is. I don't.

"I'm going to call Jackson." She says.

I stiffen, my whole body freezing into a bundle of hope, pain and fear. Jackson. His name conjures memories of a different time, a happy time, but all that has been destroyed. Whatever we had is now lost in pain and ashes.

No. My protest is desperate but silent, trapped in my head.

"Maybe you need to see him," May continues, "maybe if you tell him everything, you'll feel better."

"He won't come." I whisper. Why should he? I don't mean anything to him anymore.

"Well I'm going to try," May replies, her voice determined.

No. I make another silent protest. I'd rather die than have Jackson see me like this. I already hate myself, and how pathetic I am, but Jackson's hatred, especially when he finds out exactly what happened, it would kill me.

Nausea rises like a wave in my stomach, and I spring up from the bed, pushing past May to get to the bathroom. I retch for what seems like hours while she holds up my hair and rubs my back. It feels as if I'm letting go of everything inside me, and when I'm well and truly empty, I turn my tear-stained face towards her.

"Don't call him." I tell her.

She looks at me for a long time, and I meet her stare, letting my face convey the resolve I'm feeling. She must have seen it too, because, after a while, she nods silently and leaves me to clean up my face.

Chapter One

Present

"I know I've asked you a hundred times, but I'm going to ask one more time," May says, her voice full of friendly concern, "Do you really think you can do this?"

I let my eyes drift to the windows, where the sparkling surface of the Hudson River and the rich vegetation on the banks are rolling by at the speed of the train. In less than an hour, I'll get to my stop, only about fifteen minutes' drive to Foster, a small town on the Hudson River, where I lived from when I was fourteen to just before my eighteenth birthday.

I sigh and move the phone to my other ear. May is still waiting for me to say something. She's already in Long island, planning to spend most of the summer at the fifteen-room 'cottage' she shares with her husband Chace. I could have chosen to be there with them, taking advantage of their hospitality, enjoying a pressure free stay with friends, and teasing May about her growing belly. Instead, I'm on my way back to Foster to face a past that should stay buried.

Can I do this?

Of course, I can. I want to tell May, reassure her as well as myself. It's just another job, another high profile photo shoot in a beautiful house. I've done many of those.

Only this time, it's not just any house. It's Halcyon, the house I left seven years ago, feeling as if I would never be happy again.

"You don't have to do it, you know," May continues when I don't reply, "You could always pull the temperamental artist act and tell that editor to kiss your ass."

I laugh, despite the apprehension in my belly, as I imagine the elegant editor of American Homes, an internationally renowned architecture and design magazine, and one of the most powerful people at Gilt publications, doing anything as unsophisticated as kissing anyone's ass. "Nobody tells Grace Conlin to kiss their ass.

If I did that, I'd have to move to Montana, and maybe get a job tending horses."

"At least you'd meet some hot cowboys," May laughs. "Think of all the hard muscles and tanned skin." She sighs. "But seriously Liv, I don't think you should go back, and Chace agrees with me."

Chace and May, the only real friends I made in the four years I spent in Foster High School. They're married now, surprisingly. Two people who couldn't be more different. Where May has always been talkative and bubbly, Chace is studious and reserved. He was always a science nerd, and soon after college, it paid off when he made a lot of money from patenting some new kind of metal coating. Now he heads a private research facility where he can indulge his love for science. May is a dermatologist, one of those miracle ones that take new clients only by recommendation. Together, they make a sort of power couple, albeit being the most unlikely pairing I could have imagined back in high school.

It makes sense that they wouldn't want me to return to Halcyon. They're among the few people who know the whole story of everything I went through seven years ago. They know how long it took for me to become a fully functional person again, and they're worried about me, as real friends would be.

I yawn and look out the windows again, watching the river gleam in the late summer sun, the same river that flows through the back of the grounds at Halcyon, marking the edge of the property. I turn away from the view, closing my eyes as I fight a wave of tiredness. I've only just returned from shooting a newly renovated chateau in the south of France for a well-known magazine, and I was only able to spend a few moments in my apartment before I had to start my journey to Halcyon. I should feel lucky that I get to travel and take pictures of exotic places, but sometimes all I want to do is sleep.

"It's just a house." I tell May, "and an empty one at that. The family isn't there now. It'll just be me, and the crew from Gilt. We won't even be staying there. We have rooms at the Foster Inn for the duration of the shoot."

"Well, if you say so." She doesn't sound convinced.

"Photographing a house like Halcyon for Gilt is a wonderful opportunity for any photographer." I add reasonably, in a final attempt to convince her, or myself.

Not that it isn't. When Grace Conlin had called me about the chance to photograph Halcyon for a two hundred page book that would contain detailed articles and pictures of the most important homes in the United States, I couldn't ignore the fact that it was a great career opportunity for me. Halcyon had never been really photographed before, and I would be the first photographer to do an extensive feature on one of the most beautiful homes in the United States, for a book from a publishing giant that would grace coffee tables and libraries from New York to Timbuktu.

Yet, my first instinct had been to refuse, and I'd almost said no. The thought of returning to Halcyon and facing the people who had hurt me was enough to make me panic. I didn't want to face all those demons from my past. I didn't want to return to the scene of my disillusionment and re-live the pain again.

"Of course you should know the house belongs to Jackson Lockewood," Grace had said. She was one of those well-kept women whose age it was always impossible to guess. Her power and position however, were fully apparent as she sat across from me on her massive chrome and glass desk, with the Manhattan skyline showing through the windows behind her desk. She gave me an arch look to make sure I knew that she was talking about *the* Lockewoods. The two hundred year old dynasty that had survived the Civil War and the Great Depression, produced two presidents, three senators, successful businessmen, and at least one extremely eligible bachelor in every generation. For a moment, I wondered what she would say if I told her just how well I knew them.

"However, he doesn't live there, and neither do his sister and aunt," she had continued, unaware of the direction of my thoughts. "So it'll be just you, Elaine Black, who's writing the feature, Nick Fischer, who's in charge, and whoever else he requires to assist. The staff at the house will assist you with everything you need."

Ultimately, it was the chance to see Halcyon again without having to encounter Jackson or his family that had made me accept the job. That, coupled with the fact that nobody said no to Grace Conlin.

"I want you to be strong enough to face your memories without any problems," May is saying now on the phone, "but as your friend, I can't help being worried."

"It's just a few days." I reassure her, "and I won't be alone with my memories. Nick Fischer's in charge of the feature and the shoot, and some short fiction writer with a couple of literary prizes is writing the article. Nick will probably try to get into her pants, and whether she says yes or no, there'll be enough drama to keep my mind off my memories."

"Ah, Nick." I can almost hear May's smile. "Cute bastard."

"Bastard being the operative word," I say with a laugh. Nick Fischer is the most talented editor I know. I first met him when he was a features editor at one of the men's style magazines owned by Gilt. Since then he has risen to the position of international editor at large, with regular features in any one of the many magazines under Gilt's portfolio. When he's not trying to see if any of his lines would work on me, he can be a good friend, an effective mentor, and a perfect occasional date at work related events, but he's also a man whore to the depths of his soul. With his smooth British accent, deep pockets, and impossible good looks, women fall over themselves to get to him, and keep coming back for more regardless of how carelessly he treats them.

"Maybe you should give him a chance," May offers. "I've heard that promiscuous men like him often make ideal husbands when they settle down."

"Try telling him he's promiscuous," I say with a laugh. "He thinks the words, 'promiscuous' and 'man' are synonyms." I shake my head. "Anyway, Chace didn't have to be a man whore in the past to become an ideal husband."

I can almost hear her happy smile. "Chace is different," She says, "He was made for me."

And Jackson was made for me. I don't say it, though the words almost slip out. I shake my head, disgusted with myself. Seven years, and I still can't imagine a life with anyone else.

"Well I'm going to take a nap," May says, unaware of my thoughts, "being pregnant and all." She pauses, "All the best in Foster, Liv, and stay happy."

"I will."

Less than half an hour later, I get to my stop. Across the street from the station, there are a couple of taxis. I originally planned to take one of them to the Foster Inn, but Nick sent a text saying he'll come to the station to pick me up. He's been in Foster with Elaine Black for almost a week already, working on the story and an angle for the feature.

My phone rings and I hold it to my ear with one hand while pulling the case containing my equipment, as well as my luggage and purse with the other.

"I can see you," Nick says, his velvety voice and sexy accent filling my ears like a caress. No wonder the women could never get enough. "Just stay where you are." He continues.

I spot a deep green jaguar coming along the road. It's sleek and sexy, with a sound like the deep purr of a jungle cat. It stops right by me, and the glass rolls down, revealing Nick's dark gold curls, handsome face, and cocky smile.

He looks unbelievably hot in a dark blue polo shirt and tan trousers.

"Hey babe," He drawls. "Wanna take a ride with me?"

I burst into laughter, unable to stop even as I place my cases in the back. "I didn't know you drove a Jag." I comment, impressed. Nick is a native New Yorker, and even though I've seen him freezing in St Petersburg and wearing flowing robes in Morocco, I've never actually seen him behind the wheel of a car. "Did you steal it?" I ask, settling into the front passenger seat.

"Would that make me more attractive to you?" He

winks. "Bad boy on the wrong side of the law... Clyde to your Bonnie... Tell me that turns you on."

"Naw." I shake my head, smiling, "I'm not as adventurous as all that."

"You never know. You might like it." His blue eyes hold mine, and for a moment I wonder if he's serious, not about stealing the car, but about wanting to be attractive to me. As one of the most celebrated editors for Gilt publications, he's high up there as a force to reckon with in the world of magazine publishing. As a photographer, his patronage is invaluable to me, as a woman, it's flattering that, in all the years we've known each other, he hasn't given up on making passes at me. Nevertheless, I've never taken his attempts at seduction seriously, not when I know all about his charm'em, fuck'em, and leave'em style of dating. I'm not eager to add myself to the list of his conquests.

"I don't think so." I say with a smile.

Nick shrugs and turns back towards the road. "It's not my car." He says, in reply to my question. "Jackson Lockewood lent it to me to pick you up with."

As soon as he says the words, my heart stops, and I feel the blood drain from my face. Suddenly I can't breathe. No, I think desperately, sure that I'm going to have a heart attack. Jackson cannot be at Halcyon. I was told very clearly that he wouldn't be there. I wait for Nick to say something else, anything to show that I imagined the last sentence, but he just keeps on driving.

Suddenly, I realize that taking this assignment was a huge mistake. Because, of all the many reasons why I should never have returned to Halcyon, Jackson Lockewood is the greatest of them all.

Chapter Two

Past

I'M sitting in the back seat of my dad's SUV, engrossed in one of the romance novels my mom has given up on discouraging me from reading. My parents are in front, my dad driving, and my mom in the passenger seat, no doubt checking the rear view mirror every five seconds to see what I'm doing.

I hear them laugh, my dad's laugh is deep and resonant, my mom's, light and soft, and I pretend not to see as her hand crosses over the middle of the car to rest on his thigh. It's not moving, or doing anything gross, though it's already gross enough that it's there at all. I roll my eyes. At fourteen, I've already come to terms with the fact that my parents will never be able to keep their hands off each other, even in front of me.

Outside the car windows, the streets of Foster, the small town in the Hudson River Valley where we've recently moved, are lined with wide green trees that provide shade even in the summer. My parents think I hate it here, but I don't, at least, not as much as I've made them believe, but I do miss my old life. I miss my old school, my friends, even our old house on a street where all the houses looked almost the same.

Most times, I'd like nothing more than for my dad to decide that he doesn't want his new job managing the Lockewood Trust anymore, and move us back to our old life. But that's just wishful thinking. My dad loves his new job. He loves that he can commute to his office in New York City by train and be home in time to help my mom make dinner. My mom has also got a job at the Foster library where she can indulge her love of books, and do her freelance writing at the same time. They're happy here, and I have no choice but to swallow my discontent and try to like Foster, for their sakes.

"Honey did I mention how nice your dress looks?" I hear my Mom say.

I roll my eyes. "Yes you did Mom."

She chuckles, so I know she saw the eye roll in the

mirror. I sneak a peek and sure enough, she's looking at me. Even in the side mirror, she's really pretty. Her auburn hair is dark and wavy, and her eyes are deep green with brown flecks, or brown with green flecks depending on what she's wearing. Today, they're mostly green. People say I look like her because I have the same color of hair and eyes. But on days like this when she looks so beautiful, I find it hard to believe.

"I just don't see why I had to wear a dress, or even come at all." I complain. Constance Lockewood Milner, the chair of the board that manages Lockewood Holdings, which owns the Lockewood Trust, as well as many other Lockewood interests in finance, technology, shipping etcetera, and therefore my dad's boss, has invited us to Sunday dinner. I would have been content to stay home and finish my book while my parents went to Halcyon, the Lockewood mansion, but my mom insisted that I go with them, even making me change out of my customary jeans and sneakers as if we were on our way to a fancy restaurant in the city.

"It wouldn't hurt you to visit a historic mansion," my mom says, "and Mrs. Milner's nephew and niece are about your age." She adds, "Maybe you can be friends."

I don't reply. I don't want to remind her again that I already had my friends back home, before we were ripped apart. I miss them, Karen Pace, with her bright red hair, who never lost any weight even though she had celery for lunch every day, and Jamie Novak, who could do a perfect drawing of anyone with just a pencil or charcoal. We had our lunch together and hung out after school. We were a team. Now they'll forget about me and be a team without me, and eventually we'll become those kinds of friends whose whole friendship consist of old memories and occasional likes on a Facebook post.

"They might even let you come back and take a couple of pictures of the house," my dad adds, "wouldn't you like that?"

I shrug nonchalantly, as if I don't care, but my interest is perked. I got a camera for my tenth birthday from one of my Grans, and I've been in love with photography ever since. My parents indulge me, letting me buy all sorts of image editing software with their credit cards. I sigh. I really should be nicer about the move to Foster.

"Aren't the Lockewood children older than me?" I ask, thinking about what my mom said about us becoming friends.

"Not much," my dad replies. "Jackson is ah… eighteen and his sister Blythe is fifteen."

I shake my head. There's not much chance of older kids being even remotely interested in me. I'm neither outgoing nor funny. I'm one of those people who always have their nose in a book. I love history, poetry, and all kinds of novels. Add my obsession with taking pictures, and I'm a certified nerd. But there's no point telling my parents that. Like all loving parents, they think I walk on water, and I'm bound to be popular wherever I go.

I've never met the Lockewood children, since they don't go to the local high school, but I know from hearing some of my parents' conversations that Jackson and Blythe are the products of Constance Milner's older brother Daniel's marriage to Rachel Jackson, an oil heiress from Texas. I know that they both died when Daniel Lockewood crashed his small plane a few years after Blythe was born, killing himself, his wife and Jonathan Milner, Constance's husband. The accident left the Lockewood children orphans, but heirs to most of the combined Lockewood and Jackson fortunes.

My parents aren't poor by any standards, and they've always taught me that a person is worth more than what they have in their bank accounts, but still, the idea of meeting the Lockewoods is a little intimidating. Will they be snobbish like some of the rich kids in my new school, with their brand new convertibles and designer clothes, and total disregard for anyone not in their clique? Not that it matters, I decide, after this dinner I'll probably never see them again.

I turn back to the windows, watching as the houses get bigger, and farther away from the streets, until they are barely visible at all behind acres of lawn and trees. After a while, my Dad turns into one of the gravel covered driveways, and a pair of wrought iron gates open automatically, allowing us to drive up to the most beautiful house I've ever seen.

It's big, with a white, stone exterior that gleams in the late afternoon sun. The numerous windows reflect the sky, and the columns, arches, and carvings look like something out of the drawings of the palaces in my old fairy tale storybooks. At the end of the drive, there is a fountain, with a sculpture of a girl pouring water out of a jar. I stare, unable to comprehend that people actually live in a house that's so incredible. I've never seen anything as beautiful.

"It's lovely, isn't it?"

I tear my eyes away from the house and turn to my mom, who is smiling at me. "It's marvelous!" I exclaim, still awestruck.

"It's almost a hundred years old." My dad chips in, laughing at my rapt expression. "Kinda like your old man."

I laugh and climb out of the car, rolling my eyes as my dad rushes around to get the door for my mom. He used to get mine too, calling us his 'ladies' as he made a big show of opening car doors gallantly, but as I got older, I started scooting out of the car before he got to my side.

They hold hands as they walk towards the front door, prompting another eye roll from me before I busy myself with looking around the manicured lawns, trees, and gardens, and trying to determine where the property ends.

We only wait a few seconds at the door before it opens. I look inside, prepared to see a butler, or something else, which, like the house, does not ordinarily exist in my world, but what I see is a boy, a boy who is so stunning, he takes my breath away.

He's tall, with dark hair, parted and neatly combed. His features are perfect, wide gray eyes fringed with thick black lashes, a slim, straight nose, and sculpted lips like a male model's. He's wearing jeans and a gray sweater, with the white collar and cuffs of his shirt showing above the neckline and at the wrists of the sweater. I stare at him, immobilized, the beauty of the house fading to nothing as I lose myself in the sight of him.

"Good evening," He says politely, in a deep, cultured voice that sounds nothing like the boys I know from school. "I'm Jackson Lockewood, and you must be Mrs. Wilder, Mr. Wilder," he turns his mesmerizing eyes to me and smiles, making my blood rush to my head like a geyser, "and Olivia."

I'm too enthralled to reply. I just keep staring at him. On some level, I know I'm supposed to say something, but he's hypnotized me with his eyes, suddenly my stomach is full of butterflies, and my face feels unbelievably hot.

Luckily, my mom fills the silence. "She's Livvie to everyone but her dad," She warns with a chuckle as my dad shakes Jackson's hand. He steps back to allow my parents walk inside the house, leaving me to follow them, but I continue to stare at him. I've never met anyone so good-looking, and his gracefulness and ease are astonishing, making all the boys I know seem like snot-wiping toddlers.

When I don't move, he holds out a hand. "Come on Olivia," he says with a wink, ignoring my mom's warning about my name, "we don't want to keep them waiting."

I put my hand in his, and in that moment I know, even though I've never even had a crush before, that what I'm feeling is so much more than the adolescent fixation my friends have all experienced. I know that even though I've only just met this boy, that I want nothing more than for him to want to be with me as much as I want to be with him. I know that I would live, breathe and want only him, and even when I have him, all the time in the world would not be enough.

I'm still coming to terms with this realization when a girl bounds into the foyer, interrupting my thoughts. There is a slight resemblance to Jackson, but her eyes are blue, and her hair is the shade of honey. She sees Jackson holding my hand and groans.

"I've come to save you from my boring brother." She says with a laugh, prompting a headshake from the brother in question. "I'm Blythe," she continues, her earnest blue eyes looking right into mine.

"Livvie," I tell her, unable to understand how anybody in the world could find Jackson Lockewood boring. Even if he never said a word, I'd be content just to look at him forever.

Blythe smiles and reaches for my hand and I feel a sense of loss as Jackson lets go of my other hand.

"It was nice to meet you Olivia," He says with a small smile as Blythe pulls me into wide-open doorway of the living room, a bigger, more beautiful kind of living room than any I've ever seen. Inside, my dad is introducing my mom to a woman about my mom's age, who looks like an older version of Blythe, with light blonde hair, wide blue eyes, and a welcoming smile.

"I hear you're quite the photographer," She tells me when we're introduced. Her voice is clear and soft, and there's just something about it that draws you in and makes you feel like there's no one else she'd rather be talking to, "Halcyon hasn't been photographed in a while," She says with a smile. "Maybe you'll do us the honor?"

"I would love that!" I gush, even though I know she's probably teasing, before Blythe pulls me away to sit beside her on a two-seater sofa.

"Aunt Constance says you just moved here, and you don't know anyone," She says when we're seated. "I can't even imagine that. No matter where I go, I always seem to know hundreds of people." She looks wistful, as if she'd like to find a place where she doesn't know anyone.

"It's not fun." I tell her, thinking of all the kids I've known who didn't have any friends, and of the friends I left behind when we moved. "I'm sure it's better to have many friends."

"Yeah." She shrugs, and then beams at me. "I have a feeling we're going to be friends," she says, "All the other girls are crazy about Jackson, and it gets boring. Please tell me you won't fall for him."

Fortunately, she doesn't wait for a reply before she continues talking. I wouldn't have been able to lie, especially not when I'd already fallen for him. Blythe is a talker, barely pausing for breath before she launches from one story about her school, a private boarding school upstate, to the next. She even manages to get me talking, extracting some stories from me too. She seems sad when I tell her about missing my friends, but hopeful that I'll make new ones. I'm surprised to find myself not even missing my book, and really enjoying her company.

Every now and then, throughout the evening, my eyes would go to Jackson, on the other side of the room with my parents and his aunt, or opposite me on the formal dining table, and each time I look at him, it feels exactly like it did the first time I set my eyes on him. I feel a little lost and unlike myself, as if I'm falling down a deep well with no way to stop myself, and the only thing waiting to catch me at the bottom is him. It's a strange feeling, but I wouldn't change it for anything else in the world.

After that day, I stop missing my old life. With Blythe Lockewood as a friend, there's almost no space for melancholy or nostalgia. She's one of those girls for whom everything is effortless. She's effortlessly beautiful, effortlessly fashionable, effortlessly skilled in sports, whether on the lawn tennis court at Halcyon, or the Olympic size swimming pool. She's also incredibly sweet and sincerely friendly.

Constance Milner, or Aunt Constance as Jackson and Blythe call her, is also wonderful. She invites me to come back to Halcyon as often as I need, to take as many pictures of the house or gardens as I want, or to borrow whatever books I want from the incredible library, as long as I promise to return them. She's the kind of graceful woman I've never met before in real life, always serene and incredibly put together, putting everyone in a room at ease just by being in it.

However, it's Jackson who steals every part of my being. When I start to spend more and more time with Blythe at Halcyon during their school holidays, attending her parties, meeting her friends, and sometimes just hanging out, I really enjoy her company, but it's always Jackson I go there hoping to see.

Chapter Three

Present

"JACKSON Lockewood lent it to me to pick you up with."

My head is spinning so severely that, for a moment, I'm sure I'm going to faint. It's a good thing Nick's eyes are on the road because my face has gone white, and my hands... my whole body is trembling. I swallow and take a deep breath, increasingly sure that I must have heard him wrong."

"I'm..." I start, panic making me confused and almost incoherent, "What did you say?"

"This car drives like a dream," Nick says distractedly,

more to himself than to me, and then he seems to remember my question and turns to look at me. "Yes, it's Jackson Lockewood's, lucky bastard." He adds, before turning back to the road.

"But..." I try not to sputter, "He doesn't live at the house. He lives in the city. He's not supposed to be at Halcyon." I realize I'm beginning to sound hysterical, and I pause. "He's not there is he?" I ask, desperate and hopeful.

Nick frowns. "He is," he replies, unaware of the anxiety his words are causing me "So is his aunt, charming woman, by the way. If I weren't so in love with all things young and perky, I'd ask her to marry me."

I don't even have the presence of mind to be disgusted at Nick. That's how anxious I am. I should have listened to May, I think desperately. I should never have come back.

Just when I think it can't get worse, Nick says the words that turn my brain into a sea of pure, undiluted panic. "She invited us to stay at the house," he informs me, with a 'see, I told you she was charming' smile in my direction. "So, no nasty Foster Inn." He fakes a shudder. "Plus the cook is to die for. Just a few days and I already have a paunch." He peers at me. "Are you all right?"

For a moment, I contemplate telling him to stop the car. I want to go back to the station and back to my apartment, because right now, I'd rather lose all my credibility as a professional photographer, I'd rather never get a job again, than face Jackson Lockewood.

If I go there now, I won't be able to avoid seeing him. Even if I insist on staying at the hotel, which I really can't, not when everyone else is probably excited about spending a couple of days in a historic house that's been home to two presidents and three senators and has a spectacular cook, as long as I go on to Foster, I won't be able to avoid him. And with just his proximity, he would remind me of everything we had, and everything I lost.

Then there's also Aunt Constance. I remember the last time I saw her, and the familiar, almost constant pain is like blades tearing at my heart.

"Hello... earth to Liv Wilder."

I realize that Nick is waiting for me to say something.

"I'd have preferred a hotel." I say weakly.

He spares me a quick glance, brows raised questioningly. "I have no idea why," He remarks, "Especially when Jackson Lockewood mentioned that he was looking forward to seeing you again. For someone that hot, I'd expect you to be tearing down the gates." He smiles and gives me another quick look. "You didn't mention that you knew him. Is he my competition? The reason you're keeping me locked up in the friend zone?"

"My friend zone is a very comfortable place." I say lightly, even though my stomach is in knots. I still want to be a coward and turn back, but I know I can't do that.

Grace Conlin would probably blacklist me, and even my friendship with Nick wouldn't be able to save me then. No, Jackson has taken too much from me for me to surrender my career to him too. "You should be glad I let you in there at all," I tell Nick, "with your bad reputation."

"Well deserved." He laughs. "But still the women can't resist."

"They want to tame you," I tell him. "But I pity the one who succeeds more than the ones who fail. Imagine being stuck with you for a lifetime."

He looks hurt. "So what's the history with Jackson Lockewood?"

"Nothing," I shake my head. "I just knew him, them, the Lockewoods, when I was growing up."

"Really?" He gives me a quizzical look. "I didn't know you grew up around here."

"There's a lot you don't know about me."

"Through no fault of mine." He gives me another serious glance, and I find myself wondering again, if there's something else in his flirting. "So was he always that commanding." He asks of Jackson. "I literally felt myself fade into the background whenever he walked into the room. I think Elaine is half in love with him already, poor me. I was making some progress there before he arrived.'

I'm not really listening to him. My head is assailed with

images of Jackson. Yes, he has always been commanding, and intense, and incredibly attractive, I think silently, he has always had the power to make everything, everyone else, seem unimportant, and not just because I was hopelessly in love with him.

"I doubt anybody can make you fade into the background." I say instead.

"Then I'm sure you haven't seen your childhood friend in a while."

"No, I haven't." I reply softly. It is true. I have only seen Jackson once in the years after leaving Foster. It was my senior year in college, and I was working part time as an assistant to a popular photographer. For some reason, she'd decided I spent too much time on my own and set me up on a date with her cousin, a hotshot lawyer, who according to her, was hot, rich, and interesting.

I'd still been battling depression at the time, and still crippled by the painful memories that had made me almost drop out in my freshman year. Even though, with May and Chace's help, I had managed to catch up with my studies, get a job doing something I loved, and have a life, some days I still woke up wanting nothing more than to lie in bed forever.

I decided to go on the date as a way to fight the feelings of depression. I forced myself to take pleasure in dressing up for a man, I forced myself to care that my hair was perfect, that my clothes were perfect too. I employed every trick I'd learned about enhancing my assets, and by the time I was dressed, it was impossible for me not to take pleasure in how good I looked.

I'd been in a good mood when I walked into the restaurant. Maybe, I'd thought, I could finally forget. Maybe I could finally let go of the pain I'd been carrying around. If I liked my boss's cousin, then maybe I could have some fun. Maybe for once, I could put aside the shadow of grief and loss that had hung over me like a cloud for far too long.

I recognized my date from his picture. He was as good-looking in real life, and he looked happy to see me.

Then like a bad omen, something had changed in the air in the restaurant. I'd felt it like a tingle in my spine, a tensing of my whole body, and I'd instinctively turned my gaze, only a little, and across a table from a silky head of wavy blonde hair, staring at me with a gaze like cold steel, was Jackson.

The combination of yearning and panic was overwhelming, erasing all the thoughts I'd been having with only one. How much I missed him still, and how ashamed I was of the fact that I couldn't get over him. I had to fight the urge to go to him, tell him how much I'd missed him, to touch him, and stare forever at his face, more matured now, but still as achingly handsome as I remembered. But the disdain I saw in his eyes, the way they felt like they were stripping me of everything, my clothes, even my dignity, was too much for me. I turned and left, and I was never able to give my boss a satisfactory explanation as to why I stood her cousin up.

Even though there is a thick knot of tension in my stomach now, I doubt that seeing Jackson again would have as strong an effect as to make me run out of any room. I'm a long way from the girl who stood up her date because of one look from him. I'm a very long way from the girl who left Halcyon seven years ago, right before my eighteenth birthday. Time has healed me in many ways. I'm far from the days when I used to wish Jackson would come to find me. I'm far from the days of waking up with tears on my pillow. Years of study and work has given me some level of sophistication and thickened my skin a little. If I'm going to be in the same house with Jackson, then I'm going to smile, be cool, let him know that the past is past, and that he no longer means anything to me.

Despite my decision, I still find myself surreptitiously checking my appearance in the side mirror as we pass the gates and glide down the long driveway into Halcyon. My appearance hasn't changed a lot since I left. My dark hair has a few highlights in it courtesy of the hairdresser May drags me to once a month. Right now, it's in the high ponytail I favor when I travel. Briefly, I wonder if I should bring it down and maybe brush it, but I resist the temptation, and not just because Nick doesn't miss a thing, and I don't want to answer his questions later, but also because I'm too proud to allow myself to care about my appearance because of Jackson.

Thankfully, I'm well dressed. High-heeled black boots and perfectly fitting light blue jeans, flatter my long legs, and a dark blue cashmere top shows off my slim figure without being too clingy. I may not be wearing couture, but at least I wouldn't be facing Jackson looking like something the cat dragged in.

Nick clears the driveway, leaving the shield of the trees behind, and for the first time in seven years, I come face to face with the house I fell in love with when I was a teenager. It hasn't changed. It's still as beautiful, with the white stone walls gleaming in the sun. A little moisture gathers in my eyes and I quickly blink it away.

"I can't get over how beautiful it is," Nick is saying, uncharacteristically sober as we climb out of the car. "I can't imagine what it must be like to actually live here, can you?"

I turn from my contemplation of the house and stare at him. Before I can attempt to answer his question though, I hear the sound of the front door opening. I turn towards the sound, and immediately, my heart explodes, slamming into my ribs with a painful force as I take in the sight of Jackson Lockewood standing in the doorway, his eyes fixed on me.

I can't tear my eyes away from him. His face is chiseled, perfect, and even with his impassive expression, he's still the best thing I've seen all day.

He looks older, of course. There's no boyishness in his features now, but somehow, he looks better, every inch the handsome man he was always going to be. His shoulders are broader, and the sleeves of his pale blue shirt are folded all the way to the elbow, so I can see the strong, lean muscle of his arms. Dark gray trousers show off his narrow hips and the length of his legs. He could be a model, I think breathlessly, one of the more perfect ones, if not for the contempt in his familiar gray eyes as he looks at me.

I swallow, and tear my eyes away from him, turning to Nick, who seems unaware that even the air seems to be crackling.

"I brought her back in one piece," he says drolly, gesturing towards the car, "and Liv too," he adds with a grin. He looks from me to Jackson, as if wondering if the situation warrants an introduction. "You two have met," he states with a frown.

"Yes, of course." Jackson steps out of the doorway and walks down the stairs into the sun. His walk is a long, loose, and devastatingly sexy stride. He saunters right up to me, and smiles, momentarily disorienting me. "Welcome back Olivia," he murmurs. "How long has it been?"

He hasn't even touched me, and I can feel him, I can feel him in every cell of my body, in every inch of my skin. I pull in a breath. "Seven years," I say steadily, unwilling to acknowledge that time, three years ago in the New York restaurant.

He raises a brow, and there's a small smile playing on his beautiful lips. "Seven years then," He says. "Much too long, isn't it?" He pauses and reaches for me, and I stiffen, bracing myself for his touch, but his hand only goes up to my hair to tuck a stray strand behind my ear.

I look up at his face, searching for a clue to what he's thinking, because I'm not fooled by his apparent friendliness. I know what he thinks about me. I know that, underneath his smile and welcoming speech, he despises me.

"You look wonderful," he says, confusing me further. Of all the welcomes I had allowed myself to expect, I hadn't expected compliments.

"Thank you," I say, stepping away from him as I try to get a handle on the chaotic emotions he's awakened in just these few moments. Nick is watching us, eyebrows raised in a questioning expression. I shrug and move towards the rear door of the car, not really listening as Jackson and Nick talk about the merits of the car. I open the door and reach for my cases.

"Leave them." It's Jackson voice. So close, I almost jump out of my skin. He's right beside me, one hand resting on the roof of the car, the expanse of his chest right on a level with my eyes. "I'm sure we can have someone bring them to your room."

Even as he speaks, I can already see someone hurrying around the side of the house, coming towards us, a servant, no doubt. Someone to lift, carry, unpack, and ensure that the Lockewoods never have to lift a finger to do anything menial.

I ignore Jackson and pull out the case with my camera equipment. "I'd rather carry this myself." I say. "It's my equipment."

The next moment his fingers close over mine on the handle, sending an unbearable shock of sexual awareness coursing through me.

I pull my hand away, leaving him holding the case, and move as far away from him as I can manage without looking too skittish. My heart is pounding, and I can feel the blood rushing to my face. This is such a bad way to start my short stay in Halcyon.

"Then I'll take it." He smiles, reminding me of a wolf who knows he has his prey cornered. "You don't think I'll damage your equipment, do you?"

I shake my head, but he's already turned towards the

door, leaving Nick and me to follow. I refuse to look at Nick as we take the steps up to the front door of the house, and as I pass the very spot where I first met Jackson, I find myself wondering how on earth I'll survive a week of this.

Chapter Four

Past

"DID you know Jackson's in town?" Blythe asks, adding pink stripes to the red coat she already applied on my nails. My parents dropped me over at Halcyon for a sleepover a few hours ago, glad for an excuse to have a date night, sex on the kitchen table, or whatever they do when I'm not around. I hold my finger steady as Blythe adds a coat of glitter. I've already done hers, with red glossy polish and black half-moons at the tips. We'll clean all the colorful manicures up and go back to our sheer nail polish before we go to sleep, but it's the

41

experimentation that counts.

"No." I reply to her question, trying to keep my fingers from trembling as hope flutters in my chest. It's been a year since I first saw Jackson, but time has not diminished my reaction to him. Instead, my feelings have grown in intensity, so much that just the mention of his name is enough to start a bittersweet flutter in my chest. Even being in the same room with him is almost unbearable, and yet sweet at the same time.

I'm always happy to come over to Halcyon to hang out with Blythe, and to lose myself in the treasure of books in the library. I love to visit Mrs. Shannon, the cook, in the kitchen or the staff apartments at the end of the garden, where she allows Blythe and me to read her gossip magazines, and watch all the trash TV and reality shows we don't get to watch usually. But Jackson being around raises a visit to Halcyon from merely enjoyable to downright blissfulness.

"Is he home?" I ask, keeping my face and voice cool, "I didn't see him when I came in."

"No, he's out with Lindsay Gorman," Blythe replies matter-of-factly, unaware that the thought of Jackson with any other girl, especially one like Lindsay Gorman, with her bouncy blonde curls, perfect figure, perfect cars, and perfect clothes is like torture to me.

I swallow, and concentrate on my nails, until the colors Blythe is applying begin to fade into each other. "Is she his girlfriend?" I hear myself ask, knowing that the answer to my question may likely hurt me, but unable to stop myself.

Blythe shrugs, totally bored with the idea of her sibling's love life. "Maybe. He hangs out with her a lot," she says, unknowingly driving a knife through my chest. "But Lindsay's a first class bitch. Sometimes, I just want to wash all the makeup off her face and watch her melt like the wicked witch of the west."

I try to laugh, but there's an acute pain in my chest, so I only manage a weak chuckle.

"Her step-brother though… " Blythe continues, totally oblivious to my pain, "Carter Felton." She sighs. "I'm so in love with him, Livvie, he's just so perfect."

I listen as she tells me all the reasons why she thinks Carter might like her too, but I'm more concerned with what Jackson is doing. I torture myself with images of him with Lindsay Gorman, with the thought that they wouldn't just kiss and make out. They are both in college, practically adults, so they'll probably end their date with sex, and just the thought makes me want to cry.

"I'm going to tell him I like him." Blythe finishes, looking up at me. "I mean… I'm a modern woman, and I shouldn't wait around for a guy, right?"

"No, you shouldn't," I agree, feeling like a big hypocrite, because I know there's no way I'll ever have the guts to tell Jackson how I feel.

I wait for my nails to dry as Blythe goes to the mirror and puts on a newly acquired pair of cosmetic contacts. "How do you like my 'amber eyes'?" she asks, turning around to face me.

I'm prevented from answering by the sound of a car coming up the drive. "That's Jackson," Blythe says excitedly, "I'm going to ask him if he saw Carter." She starts towards the door. "Come on, Livvie."

As if I need an invitation. Being around Jackson, hearing his voice, and seeing that smile turned towards me turns me to a trembling, dreaming mess, but I wouldn't miss those feelings for anything else in the world.

I follow Blythe downstairs, descending the majestic curving stairs into the foyer, just as Jackson closes the front door behind him.

I take one look at him, and my stomach drops as it always does. He is breathtaking. As usual, my eagerness to see him quickly gives way to the confusion and uncertainty I always feel when he's actually around. When he looks at me, his gray eyes seem to draw me in, swallowing me. My feet fail me. My words fail me. Everything fails but my eyes, which I can't take off him.

"Did you go to Lindsay's house?" Blythe asks him, almost jumping up and down in her eagerness, and causing him to look away from me and turn towards her.

He chuckles. The sound is deep and smooth and

perfect to my ears. "No, Blythy," he replies, with a teasing note in his voice, "I didn't go to Lindsay's house, I didn't see Carter, and he didn't say anything about you."

She folds her arms. "I wasn't even asking that," she protests weakly.

He laughs and leans closer to peer at her face. "...and what happened to your eyes, Mystique?" He turns back to me. "Your eyes are lovely Olivia, no matter what Blythe does to hers, don't change yours."

Your eyes are lovely. "I won't," I manage, ignoring Blythe as she rolls the fake amber eyes. Jackson is smiling at me, igniting a sweet feeling in my belly.

"Good." He ruffles Blythe's hair playfully. "Don't let this little monster corrupt you." She ducks away with a complaint, but he ignores her. "So what have you been reading, Olivia? Have you discovered any new treasures in our underutilized library?"

I blush. Ever since he first found me in the library poring over a book of Shakespeare's sonnets, he's been teasing me about my obsession with books, even though he reads as much, if not more than I do.

"I've read a couple of good ones." I tell him.

"She's read almost all the books in there," Blythe injects. "You guys absolutely deserve each other," she adds, "Nerds United."

She means it in a teasing way, and Jackson is chuckling at the comment, but I don't laugh. The embers of hope in my chest burst into a roaring flame. If even Blythe thinks we have a lot in common, then my feelings are not so hopeless, are they?

We're still standing there when the door to the study opens, and Aunt Constance comes out into the foyer, her fingers limp around the phone she's holding. The expression of shock and sadness on her usually serene face is a sure sign that something is wrong.

"Livvie..."

As soon as she says my name, I know something bad has happened. I take a step towards her and look past her into the study. Through the open door, I can see the TV turned on to a local news channel. There's no sound, but the headline is written on the screen. Local couple killed by drunk driver.

Immediately, I know it's my parents. I feel my heart disappear to be replaced by something raw and aching. I hear someone screaming, and I realize that it's me. I start to sob, closing my eyes to block out Aunt Constance's red eyes and Blythe's sad confusion. My body is shaking so hard, I can barely stand, and just before my legs give way, strong arms encircle me, and Jackson's voice is whispering in my ear, soothing and comforting. "Shhhh," He says softly, "It's going to be all right."

The Lockewoods support me through the awful days that follow, the funeral, the lawyers and the banks, and the liquidation of my parents assets to create a fund that would support me, not luxuriously but adequately, through high school and college and maybe beyond. The last of my grans died a few months ago, and since, like me, my parents were both only children, I don't have any close relatives to take me in. Aunt Constance insists that I stay at Halcyon, and after everything is over, she offers to be my guardian until I turn eighteen.

I was in love with Jackson before, but after he took me in his arms and wiped my tears on the worst day of my life, I became his devoted slave. He never treats me as anything more than a little sister, so I have to content myself with my fantasies and my daydreams, where he always plays the lead role.

The year after my parents die, Blythe starts to go out with Carter Felton, and then leaves for college. I'm left with Aunt Constance, Mrs. Shannon and the other housekeeping staff. Aunt Constance works most of the time, remaining in the city for about three days every week to fulfill her responsibilities as the chair of the board of Lockewood Holdings, a position she holds in trust for Jackson, so I'm mostly alone in the big house.

I spend my free time exploring. I find the paintings and antique furniture in the attic, the rock bed that separates the lawns from the waterfront, and the assorted collection of sculptures in the garden. There's also an artificial pond, overgrown with lilies, at the end of the gardens that was added by Tippy Lockewood, the great-grandmother whose husband, Edward Lockewood, was a former president. I explore the second floor balconies from where I can see the river for miles, as well as the towering skyline of the city in the distance. My best discovery is the gazebo beside the lily pond, with the colorful flower boxes and cushioned seats along the circular walls, and it becomes my favorite spot in the whole house.

All the beauty of the house pales in comparison to Jackson though, By the time I turn sixteen I'm so obsessed with him, my greatest fear is that somehow he'll find out and not want me. So even though he's the main character in all my fantasies, even though I'm so crazy about him I don't go a second without thinking of him, I keep my feelings to myself, while spending many agonizing hours imagining him with Lindsay Gorman.

Chapter Five

Present

I walk behind Jackson into the familiar foyer. It's still as beautiful as in my memories, with the sparkling crystal chandelier hanging down from the ceiling, and the wide curving stairs leading to the upper floor.

I sigh, and shut down the nostalgia threatening to overwhelm me, instead concentrating on the sight of Jackson walking ahead of me. He's holding my case as if it weighs nothing, his stride as confident and easy as if he were holding nothing at all. The years have been kind to him I reflect, magnifying his attractiveness to the point where it is impossible not to be overwhelmed by it. He has used it to his advantage, the combination of his looks, money and social pedigree. According to the gossip columns, he's one of the most eligible bachelors in New York society, and I've never seen a picture of him at some society event without a beautiful woman on his arm.

He's has also proven himself to be a sound businessman. According to what I've read about him, he has more than doubled the size of the Lockewood holdings since he took over. With his looks, money and business acumen, as well as his keen intelligence, he's the kind of man people write books about.

He stops at the door to the living room and turns around, catching me staring. I look away, busying my eyes with the pattern on the marble floors while he opens the door and waits for me to go in ahead of him.

"Jackson." I hear the voice from my past right before I enter the room and see aunt…no, just Constance, setting a book aside, and getting up from an armchair. Time has been kind to her as well, but when is it ever unkind to people with the kind of money she has? She still has that serene beauty I spent most of my youth admiring and trying to emulate. Her beautiful hair is held up in a French knot, and her clothes are immaculate. As she looks at me, her gaze softens. I look away from her face, unwilling to remember, to think of anything that will cause me pain.

"Livvie, my dear," She comes forward to give me one of her sweet smelling hugs, followed with soft kisses on both my cheeks. "Look how beautiful you've grown."

I don't like how like a reunion it all feels, first Jackson, now Constance, but I shelve the feeling for a moment to return Constance's hug. "Thanks," I reply, "and you don't look a day older."

She laughs. "Now you sound like Nick."

"God forbid," I say, ignoring Nick's hurt expression.

"I haven't said anything that wasn't true," He says in his defense, directing one of his charming smiles at Constance, "and I didn't know how well you all knew each other. I'm beginning to think of this as some sort of a reunion."

"Oh, it is." Constance looks from me to him, "Didn't Livvie tell you she grew up here?"

"In this house?" Nick looks incredulous as he turns a questioning glance at me, "Liv?"

"Apparently, that's not information '*Liv*' shares with her *friend*s." Jackson's voice is mocking, with an inflection of the word 'friend' that makes me wonder if he thinks perhaps that there's something going on between Nick and me. He's still standing by the door, leaning on the polished wood frame and looking at me with a slightly mocking smile. After a quick glance at him, I direct my gaze back to Constance. Even if there were anything between Nick and me, it wouldn't be any of his business.

"You must be tired after your journey," Constance says, ending the awkward silence that follows Jackson's words, "Elaine and Carl are in the library looking through some old family history, but I suppose you would rather go to your room and freshen up than join them right now."

"I am tired," I reply, thinking I would rather rest than spend time with a writer I've never met and Nick's assistant, whom I don't know very well.

Constance nods, "Well, I'll get Sara to show you to your room." She pauses. "We've put you in the east wing with the rest of your team."

Her eyes are on my face, looking uncertain, as if she's worried that I may not be happy about the choice of room.

"Thank you Constance," I reply with a gentle smile. It's not as if I was eager to stay in the family wing with Jackson just doors away.

"There's no need for Sara." I hear Jackson's say. "I'll show her up to her room." He taunts me with a smile in my direction, "I may as well complete the job of transporting her delicate equipment."

I open my mouth to protest. The last thing I want is to go upstairs with Jackson, to be alone with him, even for a moment. Only now, there's no way to avoid it without sounding unreasonable.

I can't afford to be unreasonable, or to give Jackson a reason to suspect that I'm afraid to be alone with him. I square my shoulders. What's the worst that could happen anyway?

"We'll catch up when you come down for dinner," Constance whispers, before I leave her and go to the door, towards Jackson, who's watching me as if I'm his prey. He follows be back into the foyer, and when we're alone, it's all I can do to prevent the tension I'm feeling from showing on my face.

His gaze is sardonic as he looks at me. "You know the way," he says.

I turn towards the grand staircase, trying to forget that he's walking behind me as I ascend to the second floor. I know the way to the east wing, but I have to wait for him to go ahead of me and open the door to one of the many bedrooms. It's one of the larger rooms, with the walls and décor mainly in a soft dusky pink. It's beautiful, grander than my old room, or any room I've stayed in all my life for that matter.

Jackson puts the case down by the bed, and turns to watch me as I walk inside.

"Thank you," I say, not looking at him, but hoping that he'll take the hint and leave.

"My pleasure."

Hasn't it always been about that! I think resentfully. I was here for his pleasure when I was a silly child who didn't know better, thinking that I was in love, and when he'd had his pleasure, it had been easy for him to discard me as if I was nothing. I close my eyes against the memories, banishing them from my mind.

He doesn't make any move to leave, so I move farther inside the room, away from him and towards the windows. Outside, I can see the length of the driveway, before the curtain of trees that prevents me from seeing it all the way to the gate. The gardens are also visible, as well as the fountain in front of the house. I keep my eyes on those, waiting to hear the sound of the door closing so I can know for sure that he has left me alone.

"If you're wondering where Nick is staying," I hear Jackson say, the sound of his voice dispelling my hope that he would leave, "He's only a couple of rooms down the hall."

I almost laugh. So he does think that I and Nick have something going on... well I am not going to deny it. Let him think what he wants. "Okay," I reply, keeping my face blank as I turn around to face him, let him interpret it any way he wants.

He moves towards me. Just a step, but my heart skips a beat, then resumes with a speed that makes me start to feel lightheaded. "So are you two together?" He asks lightly.

"Do you ask all your guests about their sex lives?"

He chuckles. "So you're not sleeping with him?"

I sigh, "It's none of your…"

"Why did you come?" He interrupts me. "Why did you come back here?"

I've been asking myself that question since I found out that he was here.

I shrug. "I got a job."

"And do you never refuse a job?"

I meet the storm in his gray-eyed gaze. "I couldn't refuse this one, Jackson. And anyway, I didn't realize that you'd be here."

He tilts his head slightly as he considers me. "So you'd have turned it down if you'd known I'd be here."

"Probably," I reply.

"Why? I thought it was a job you couldn't refuse." His voice is mocking as he throws my words back at me. "Are you afraid of me?"

"I am not." Even as I say the words, I realize that I'm lying. I am afraid of him, but I'd rather die than let him know that. "I'm just not eager to revisit ancient history."

"And yet here you are at Halcyon."

"I would gladly have stayed at the hotel," I tell him, "I'm only here because you invited us to stay."

"I didn't," He informs me drily, "For whatever reason Constance thought it was a good idea."

So he hadn't wanted me here either. Well I don't care. "It's only for a few days," I say dismissively. "I don't believe the past matters enough to make it impossible for us to coexist under the same roof."

"No, it doesn't." He agrees. "It doesn't matter at all."

Why does it hurt, I wonder, that he has so casually dismissed a part of my life that has influenced almost every decision I've made since then. I turn away from him, back towards the windows, because I don't want him to see the moisture brightening my eyes. I wish he would leave, and give me some time to get my armor up. I'm going to need it if I'll have to live with him in the same house for the next few days.

I don't hear him move towards me, not until he's standing mere inches away from me. My body tenses at his nearness. I want to move far away from him, to put some distance between us, but my traitorous body is remembering what it felt like to be touched by him, and yearning, almost desperately for even the small gap between us to be filled.

By sheer force of will, I keep looking out of the windows, pretending that I can't feel him standing so close, ignoring the heat building inside me, the hunger as every surface of my skin screams for him to touch me,

"Constance is right," he murmurs, his deep voice so close to my ear, that I can feel his warm breath tickle my neck, "You have grown very beautiful."

I don't trust myself to speak, not when he's so close. I don't trust myself not to do something foolish and undo all the closure I've managed to get in the seven years I've been away from him. I search my head frantically for anything to occupy my mind, to take it away from the memories of how his touch used to feel, and thoughts of how it would feel now.

When I'm sure I have my insane desires under control, I turn to face him. "I'm glad you think so Jackson," I say bravely, my expression blank as I look squarely into his eyes. I can do this, I think triumphantly, I can handle him. "Thank you," I finish dismissively.

He chuckles softly and reaches up, the small movement making me flinch, half in anticipation and half in uncertainty, as my bravery of a few moments ago, flees me. I don't know what he means to do, but I'm sure I don't want his hands anywhere on me, because God knows I'm neither strong enough, nor indifferent enough for that.

He strokes a thumb across the base of my throat, where my pulse is beating a rhythm against the surface of my skin. His finger is warm and firm, and just that slight touch does things to my body, things that have nothing to do with self-control, and everything to do with the sexy, extremely attractive man standing in front of me.

"Am I making you nervous?" he asks, his voice beguilingly intimate.

I shake my head. "No."

"Your heart is racing," he murmurs, tracing his thumb down from my collarbone towards the neckline of my top. I should tell him to stop. I want to. I want to walk away, slap his face, tell him to get the hell out of my room, but something keeps me rooted to the spot. His abandons my neckline, and trails a light path down my arm with his fingers, and despite myself, I tremble slightly at the contact.

I drag in a shaky breath, my mind unwilling to accept that even though I haven't been this close to him in seven years, with just one touch, my body is already consumed with wanting him.

"What are you doing, Jackson?" I say shakily. "What are you trying to prove?'

There is no humor in his smile. "Perhaps I'm just wondering if underneath that cool exterior you're as indifferent to me as you seem to be."

"What does it matter if I am or not?" I ask. "I'm only here to work."

"Not to revisit ancient history, as you've already said." His hand comes up to draw a soft line across my cheek. The touch is gentle, almost tender. "And you have no interest in renewing old friendships, and mixing business with pleasure."

I laugh. It's a short bitter sound. "If it's you offering the pleasure, then I'll pass. Thank you." I shake my head. "I've had enough of your particular brand of pleasure to last me a lifetime."

He considers me for a moment. "Well if not me, you

could always find someone else to play with. You were always very resourceful at finding unsuspecting guys to seduce, weren't you?"

I flinch at his words as memories fight their way into my head through the walls I've kept up for seven years. If only he knew, I think bitterly. "I'm not going to join you in talking about the past, Jackson. I've moved on."

He shrugs and steps back, as if our conversation had never happened. "Blythe will be here sometime during the week. I have no idea how long she's staying."

Blythe too! I sigh. This is becoming more and more like a reunion every minute.

"And you?" I ask, "Do you plan to remain here for long?"

"Would you rather I left?"

"It's your house." I say with a dismissive shrug.

An eyebrow goes up. "So it doesn't matter to you if I'm here or not?"

"No." I lie.

He moves towards me again, and I stiffen, my heart hitting my ribs hard as he leans over me. There is a dangerous gleam in his eyes, but otherwise there's no expression on his face. I want to step back from him, but at the same time, I want him to do something, to touch me, to remind me why I've only ever really wanted him.

"How easily you dismiss me." He murmurs. "I should warn you that I'm not so nonchalant about your presence here. Frankly I don't know if I want to hurt you for coming back here after everything, or fuck you till your body can't take anymore."

The image pushes its way into my head and immediately my foolish body clenches in response. I swallow hard, but I don't move, and neither does he. I want to say something dismissive, some careless remark about his last statement, something to put him in his place, but words fail me. Maybe if he weren't standing so close, maybe if his eyes weren't burning a hole in me, maybe if I didn't actually want him to lean a little closer and remind me of what his lips feel like. Maybe then, I could find the right words.

A discreet knock on the door brings me to my senses. I step back from Jackson just as the door opens, and a young man walks in carrying the rest of my luggage.

"Well, enjoy your stay," Jackson says, as if we've only been having a friendly conversation, then he turns and walks out of the room, leaving it feeling strangely empty in his absence.

Chapter Six

Past

THERE'S a lot of noise in the pool area, loud shrieks followed by splashes whenever one of the girls gets pushed into the water. I've already been pushed in twice, once by Blythe, and once by her boyfriend Carter. It may have been my imagination, but I think his hands lingered at my waist for far too long.

It's one of those summer parties that start out of nothing. Usually Blythe hanging out with some friends and then more and more people show up until it's a pool party.

They're usually fun, and this one is no different. I'm sitting at the edge of the pool, feet in the water, having an argument with May, my best friend from school, and Lettie Lockewood, Jackson and Blythe's second cousin who's staying for the summer, about how reading books is so much better than watching the movies made about them.

"I want to be a doctor, so I've been reading Gray's anatomy since when I was ten," May says, "I watch movies to rest my brain, and I don't have the time to read anything else."

"I watch Grey's Anatomy." Lettie says softly. She's like a thinner, younger, and shyer version of Blythe. Her mother is a reclusive artist who never married, and according to Blythe, even Lettie doesn't know who her real father is. "I also read," she continues, "but none of the books I read ever gets made into movies."

I laugh, thinking of the stack of romance novels she brought with her to Halcyon. "Nobody's going to make a movie based on a romance novel." I say.

"Why not?" She complains.

I'm about to reply when the doors to the terrace open and suddenly Jackson is standing there.

He's been spending the summer in the city, interning at an investment firm and staying at the family's Park

Avenue apartment. I've missed him all summer, and now, seeing him, I feel as if I've slammed into something hard. I want to run over and throw my arms around him. I'm overwhelmed by a mixture of delirious happiness and tense confusion. I want so much, but I'm not even sure what exactly I want.

He's wearing a white short-sleeved shirt and knee length shorts, a pair of dark sunglasses perched on his hair. I watch him, unbelievably tense as he scans the pool, his eyes coming to rest on me.

For a moment, it's just us. I lose myself in his gaze. My heart stops and my skin flushes, suddenly hot and cold at the same time. I don't know how long we're like that, but someone calls his name and he looks away.

I breathe, wetting my lips as I wait for my heart to return to its normal rate. I watch as Lindsay Gorman, wearing a tiny scarlet string bikini, leaves the lounge chair where she was lying and runs to throw her arms around Jackson, planting a kiss on his lips, no doubt eager to display their intimacy to the whole world.

I look away, determined not to be hurt. She's his girlfriend, or on again - off again girlfriend, as Blythe unrepentantly says to her face. Of course, they kiss. Of course, they're intimate. It's none of my business what they do together.

At times like this, I wish I was older and more

confident, then maybe I would be brave enough to tell him how I feel without being so afraid of what it would mean if he doesn't feel the same way.

Blythe comes out of the pool, soaking wet, but looking amazing in a black bikini, with her wet hair hanging down her back. She only has time to call out a greeting to her brother before she gets pushed back inside the pool. She emerges moments later to chase the culprit around the terrace, prompting laughter from everyone, but I can't bring myself to join in the merriment.

I sneak another look at Jackson and Lindsay. She's pulled him towards her lounge chair, and they're standing beside it, her body plastered against his as she whispers something into his face.

I watch them, filled with an acute and painful jealousy, I don't know how long I stare, but suddenly Jackson turns his face and looks right at me, and I freeze.

I don't know if he sees the hurt and jealousy written plainly on my face, and at that moment, I don't care. Lindsay follows his gaze and turns around to look at me. Her eyes narrow and I flush, looking away.

May and Lettie are still talking, but I'm not interested anymore. I mumble some inane excuse to them and pick up my towel, getting up to go into the house. I'd rather be upstairs in my room reading a book than have to watch Jackson make out with his idiotic girlfriend.

I go into the house, leaving the noise and the sun behind as I move towards the stairs. I don't go very far before I hear the door to the terrace open behind me.

"Hey, Livvie…" I turn around to see Lindsay coming into the house behind me. "It's Livvie, isn't it?" She continues sweetly, "I always forget."

I bite back a sarcastic retort about memory loss. "Do you want something?" I ask politely.

"Yes actually." She smiles, but it doesn't reach her eyes. "Some loser poured a drink on my towel. Can you get me another one?"

I shrug and go to the linen closet. It's close to the back of the house, beside the laundry and the kitchen. I'm surprised to hear her footsteps following behind me. I open the closet and retrieve a fresh towel, when I close the doors she's standing right beside me.

"Here." I hand it to her.

She reaches for it, and then pauses without taking it from me. Her pretty eyes are hard and unfriendly as she looks at me. "You think Jackson is hot, don't you?"

"Excuse me?"

"I've seen the way you look at him," she continues, as if she didn't hear me, "I'm sure you think it's really convenient that you live in his house." She smiles tightly. "Just don't forget that he's mine."

She's looking at me with a challenge in her eyes. I

almost pity her, because I know how insecure she must be to confront me like this. "If he were yours you wouldn't need to warn me off him." I say frankly.

Her face contorts in an expression of scorn. "Do you think I'm the only one who's noticed how your eyes follow him around? You're making everyone uncomfortable and making a fool of yourself. Even Jackson's noticed and he feels sorry for you. Why do you think he spends so much time away?"

I keep my eyes square on her face, determined to hide the flood of pain that's threatening to drown me. From her satisfied expression, I can tell she knows that she's hit her mark. At that moment, I hate her more than I've ever hated anyone or anything in my life.

"Do you want the towel?" I ask calmly.

She looks as if she wants to say something else, but after a moment, she snatches the towel from my hand and flounces away.

Summer passes, and in the fall, Blythe goes back to school, and once more I'm left practically alone in the big house with only Mrs. Shannon for company.

"Where have you gone?"

"What…?" I snap out of my thoughts to see Mrs.

Shannon watching me from the other side of the kitchen island. She's a plump, good-natured woman somewhere around middle age, and right now, she's watching me with a frown on her face.

"I thought you said you wanted to learn how to bake a pie," She says, shaking her head and going back to kneading the lump of dough on the board. "All you've done is sit there on that stool and stare into space."

"I'm sorry." I sigh, "I just have a lot on my mind."

"At your age?" She chuckles. "Like what?"

Like my conversation with Lindsay, which I haven't stopped thinking about since it happened. Like Jackson. Ever since that day at the pool, there's been some sort of subtle shift in our relationship. He hardly came home through the rest of the summer, and when he did, it was almost as if he didn't want to be anywhere around me. I had no choice but to conclude that Lindsay was right. He can see my stupid obsession with him written on my face, and he'd rather avoid me than watch me continue to make a fool of myself.

"Now you've gone off again." Mrs. Shannon shakes her head, "You're not learning anything here. Maybe you should go take some pictures with that camera of yours, or better yet, you can go pick me some apples."

There's an apple orchard adjoining the property. It's called the Lockewood orchard, even though it's owned by the town and not the family. Every fall, a lot of people go there to pick apples and enjoy the outdoors.

"I've never been to the apple orchard."

"Why not?" She exclaims. Her eyes go to something behind me at the door. "Jackson," she calls, making my head snap back towards the door, and sure enough, Jackson is standing there. I didn't even know he was home. I catch myself before I make a fool of myself by staring at him and betraying the all-consuming yearning I feel for him. After a quick hello, I hastily turn back to Mrs. Shannon.

"Livvie says she's never been apple picking." She tells him, unaware of the hard knot my stomach has become, and the tension that has taken over my body. "You should take her."

"He doesn't have to." I say quickly. If he's trying to avoid me, then I'm not going to force myself on him. "I'm sure Jackson is busy, and I can manage by myself."

Mrs. Shannon gives me a queer look. I can feel Jackson's eyes on my back. I cringe, embarrassed and desperately wishing I could just disappear.

"I remember when you used to get so excited at the prospect of going over to the farms to pick apples you'd almost throw up." Mrs. Shannon says to Jackson. If it's supposed to make me laugh, it doesn't work, but I hear Jackson's chuckle. I sneak a look at him, and he's leaning on the doorframe, looking amused.

"What do you say, Olivia?" He says, his mesmerizing smile turned toward me. 'Shall we go pick some apples before my inner child gets overexcited and starts throwing up?"

I nod slowly, despite all my reservations, very ecstatic at the thought of spending time with him. "I'll just get a jacket." I say, getting up from the kitchen stool.

"Don't bother," he says easily, shrugging off his jacket and handing it to me, "You can wear mine."

I put it on gratefully. It smells like him, light cologne mixed with a scent that's just him. I would have liked to go up to my room, brush my hair and maybe apply lip-gloss, but getting to wear Jackson's jacket makes up for losing the chance to do all that.

Mrs. Shannon is looking at me with a queer expression. I realize I'm hugging the jacket close to me, and I free it quickly.

"Don't forget to get me some apple cider." She says.

"Okay," I reply, following Jackson to the door.

Outside, it's a little cold, and the view from the house to the river is dotted with trees that are already red and gold with the season. It's beautiful as usual, and the reason why the valley was such a popular retreat for wealthy New Yorkers back in the day. Jackson also takes a moment to admire the view, breathing in the clean, crisp air and giving me a small smile before starting to walk towards the gardens and the trees beyond. A fence separates the farm from the estate, with a tiny iron gate. It's not locked, and Jackson reaches through the bars to move the bolt, opening it.

"I didn't know you were coming home." I say, as he holds the gate open for me to step onto the stone path that leads to the farmhouse.

"Yeah," he shrugs, "I have some friends who think weekends are meant for partying until we pass out. This weekend I'm taking a breather from roommates who are either puking or nursing a massive hangover."

I giggle. "So you abandoned them to their fate."

"Yes, I'm an awful friend." He says with a laugh.

"No, you're not." I reply earnestly.

He smiles at me but doesn't reply. At the farmhouse, we get the cider, a box, and a picker pole.

"My dad used to bring us here when we were little," He says, "Me, Blythy, and my mom." A shadow crosses his features, and I realize he must be thinking about his parents. They're dead, like mine.

"Why is it called the Lockewood orchard?" I ask Jackson, as we move through the trees. The sweet smell of autumn and apples is thick in the air. I take a deep breath and smile shyly at him.

"It used to be part of the Lockewood estate," he says

carelessly, using the pole to pluck an apple from the top of a nearby tree. "The first Lockewood who lived here was a farmer. His son rebelled and went into the ferry business. He made a huge fortune in transportation, and when his father died he gave some of the farmland to the town, tore down the farmhouse, and built the old house." He looks at me, "Are you bored yet?"

As if. "I'm not," I reply. I'd seen old sepia tinted pictures of the old house in the library. "What happened to the old house?"

Jackson leans the pole against a slender tree trunk and pauses to roll back the cuffs of his shirt. For a moment, I forget what I asked him and just enjoy looking at him.

"There was a fire around the turn of the century, and it burned to the ground."

"Oh, that's awful."

"Yeah," he shrugs, "My great, great, great grandfather built Halcyon," He looks at me. "You know what it means?"

"Heavenly," I tell him.

"Yeah," He picks an apple off a low branch, and places it inside the box I'm carrying, then he takes the box from me. "Heavenly house." He smiles again, making me forget that I should be trying to hide how I feel about him. I stare at him, mesmerized, "I'd forgotten how much of a nerd you are." He says with a teasing note in his voice.

I don't bother to deny it. "I wondered about it, so I looked it up. I couldn't find any information about the farms though, and the old house."

"Why didn't you ask me?"

I busy myself with picking a few low hanging apples. During the summer, I'd been convinced that he was avoiding me. There was no way I'd have asked him anything. I turn to place the fruit inside the box he's holding, and he's looking at me intently, waiting for me to say something.

"You hardly spoke to me all summer." I blurt.

When he doesn't say anything, I start to babble. "Lindsay said you were avoiding me because it was so obvious I had a crush on you and you didn't want me to keep making a fool of myself whenever you were around."

His expression is one of disbelief. "Lindsay said what?" He drops the box on the grass, "and you believed her?"

I swallow. "It felt like you were avoiding me."

He sighs. "Lindsay has no idea how I feel about anything," He says, "Okay?"

I nod, confused. He picks up the box and starts to walk back towards the gate. I follow him, half exhilarated that I was wrong about him avoiding me, and half embarrassed because I've just told him that I have a crush on him. Well at least he hasn't said anything about that.

At the gate, he pauses and turns to look at me. "So do you have a crush on me?" His tone is teasing, but his eyes are serious. I flush, embarrassed at having revealed something I've kept so close to my chest for years. A crush doesn't even begin to describe what I feel for him.

I want to say yes, but something holds me back. For the past few weeks I've been determined to keep my feelings to myself, and for some reason, even though now I know Lindsay was lying, it still feels risky to let him know the extent of all the things I feel for him, after all, for whatever reason, he did keep his distance throughout the summer.

"Everybody my age has a crush on something or someone." I say, with a flippant note in my voice.

He chuckles. "That's fair." He opens the gate and lets me through. I wait as he puts the bolt back into place, then he turns to me.

"Olivia." He says.

"Yes."

"I think you're sweet, beautiful, and intelligent. You're an awesome girl, and if you had a crush on me, I wouldn't think you were making a fool of yourself. I'd feel honored."

There's an erratic fluttering where my heart should be.

I stare at him, unable to say anything through my dazed happiness. He doesn't wait for me to say anything though. He keeps on walking, carrying the box full of apples, leaving me to follow him back to the house with a stupid grin on my face.

Chapter Seven

Present

I unpack my clothes, mentally trying to compose myself. I have only about an hour until dinnertime, so I manage a shower and a quick nap before brushing out my hair and pulling on a flattering deep green shirtdress, with a belted waist and a hem that's just above my knees. It's not too dressy, but it's not casual either and seems suitable for the semi-formal dinner arrangement that's always been the style at Halcyon.

I let my hair hang down around my shoulders, and

after a moment's hesitation, I apply a little makeup. Somewhere inside, I know I'm taking such care with my appearance because of Jackson. I hate myself for caring how he sees me. I really shouldn't, not after everything.

I descend the grand curving stairway, remembering all the times when I went up and down the same stairs as a teenager. I trail my fingers down the smooth wooden banister, which is polished to perfection, and gleams richly in the lights from the chandelier. I study the patterned marble floors of the foyer, the paintings hanging on the walls, the fresh flowers from the garden on the side tables, and I'm consumed by wistfulness. With nobody else in the room to remind me of how much time has passed, I can almost believe that things haven't changed at all and that I'm still the child who was so happy here.

However, I'm not, I'm a grown woman now, and I'm here to do a job. In the time since Jackson left my room, I've toyed with the idea of calling Grace and telling her to find a replacement. I've tried to come up with excuses to give her, but it's no use. There's nothing I can tell her that won't make me seem immature and unprofessional.

I hear the voices coming from the main living room

before I get to the door. I pause, listening to the muted sounds of laughter and conversation. I can't hear Jackson's voice, but I imagine that he's in there. I imagine his eyes looking up as soon as I enter the room, and looking over me with that mixture of insolence and disdain I've come to expect from him. I smooth the front of my dress, my sudden nervousness followed by disgust at myself for letting the thought of him affect me so much. Annoyed, I turn away from the door and find my way to the kitchen.

I'm surprised by the rush of emotion I feel when I see Mrs. Shannon working at the kitchen island, putting the finishing touches to the dinner she's prepared. I pause at the door, watching her work and blinking away the moisture gathering in my eyes. I can't believe how much I've missed her, and I can't believe it's been seven years since I last saw her.

Suddenly she stops working and notices me at the door, and to my relief, her face breaks into a huge, welcoming smile. "Oh my... Livvie." She exclaims, wiping her hands on her apron as she comes round the island towards me.

I hurry to meet her, and she wraps me in a warm hug. It's overwhelming, the relief I feel. I wasn't sure how she would receive me, especially since I never bothered to contact her all these years. I was so heartbroken when I left that I closed my heart to everything that had anything to do with Halcyon, everything that had the potential to remind me of Jackson, and everything I had lost.

She releases me then steps back to look at me. "Look how you've grown!" She exclaims, "and as skinny as a bone too."

"I'm far from skinny." I reply with a laugh. "Don't tell me you're still trying to fatten everyone up?"

"What's the point of my job if people don't eat?" She grumbles. "Anyways, the house is empty a lot these days. There's no one but myself and the rest of the staff to fatten."

"So the family really doesn't live here anymore?"

She goes back to the island, putting on a pair of oven mitts, as I wonder if she'll respond to my question. I wonder if she's deciding whether I still deserve to be confided in, now that I'm practically a stranger. "Mrs. Milner comes about once a month, but she lives in her house at Rhode Island now. Blythe stores her clothes here, but she's mostly in the city."

What about Jackson? I manage to keep myself from asking the question, waiting impatiently, as she bends to retrieve a perfect looking steak from the oven.

"Jackson though… he's hasn't been here in a long time. I was surprised when he arrived yesterday. It's been a while since I saw him outside the pages of the society columns."

"Oh." Then Grace Conlin had been right about the house being empty. It usually was, but for some reason, my arrival had coincided with the family suddenly deciding to show up.

"Well, a lot's changed." Mrs. Shannon looks at me. "I learned you're photographing the house for a book about great houses?"

I nod.

"Well, that's a good thing, I guess." She says, "If the house ends up with the National Trust, future Lockewoods can read all about it."

She doesn't sound very happy about it, and her tone alarms me. "Is that… is Jackson planning to give the house away?" I don't even want to think about it. While, on one hand, it would be nice to open up such a beautiful house to the public, on the other hand, what would happen to the ties the family has to their home? I would sink every last penny I had into keeping Halcyon if it were mine.

Mrs. Shannon only shrugs in reply.

I watch as she continues to work, my mind in

turmoil. Why would Jackson even want to give up the house? It's not as if he doesn't have the money to maintain it.

"Jackson would never let Halcyon go." I say firmly, wishing it more than believing it.

"Well." Mrs. Shannon sighs. "I don't know." She pauses. "It was really nice to see you again Livvie."

"Me too." I say truthfully.

"I'm looking forward to having you around again," She says, "just don't try to come into my kitchen and make cupcakes, or whatever it is you're crazy about cooking now." We both laugh. "Let them know dinner is ready, okay? And try to eat something, so my hard work doesn't go to waste."

When I return to the living room, the conversation and laughter is still going on. Constance is sitting beside Nick on a sofa. On his other side, a rail thin girl with striking red lips and raven black hair styled in a severe bob is sitting with her long supermodel body stretched out gracefully. She's laughing at something Nick is saying, as is Constance. Across from them, on an armchair, Nick's assistant Carl looks on, with a smile of amusement. He's as dark as Nick is fair, with coffee skin, dark gray eyes, and short curly hair.

As I hover by the door, Constance turns to him.

"That didn't really happen, Carl, did it? Your boss is pulling our legs"

"Oh, it did." Carl says earnestly, making me wonder which one of Nick's tall tales he's been relating. Aside from the four of them though, the room is empty.

Constance notices me at the door. "Here you are! I'd started wondering if I'd have to come get you. Did you have a nice rest?"

"Yes." I walk in to the room and take a seat next to Carl. "I went to see Mrs. Shannon too."

"Oh, good." Constance smiles, "You were always very fond of her."

I return her smile. "Well she said to tell you dinner is ready."

"Perfect then, we'll go eat in a few minutes."

"You haven't met Elaine Black, have you Liv?" Nick drawls. "She's writing the feature."

Elaine smiles. She looks very young, at least a few years younger than me, but her blood red lips and hairstyle make her look slightly cruel. "Actually, Nick and I are working on the feature together," She says in a soft and smoky voice, looking me up and down with sharp green eyes. "I hear you used to live here, in this house."

"I did," I reply.

"How nice for you."

"Yes, how nice." I say drily.

"Livvie…" Constance starts, then smiles softly before continuing. "Liv lived here for four years after her parents died." She explains to Elaine.

"Oh." Green eyes turn back to me. "I'm sorry about your parents."

I shrug. "It was a long time ago."

She turns back to Constance. "Jackson said he would show me the original plans for the house and the gardens tomorrow."

Constance nods. "That makes sense. They're stored somewhere in the study, I think."

"Yes." Elaine is smiling as she turns back to me. "He's also going to take me through the grounds. Apparently, there are stories behind some of the sculptures in the garden that might be useful for our feature."

Is she saying all this for my benefit, to let me know that she has laid claim to Jackson's time? Well she can have him. I don't care what Jackson does or with whom he does it. It's none of my business. I've passed the stage where a picture of him in a magazine with a woman on his arm could reduce me to tears.

"How fascinating," Nick says. "I'd like to see the

plans and hear all about the sculptures too, Elaine. When's Jackson available tomorrow."

I don't hear what she says in reply. There's a movement at the door, and I look towards it, expecting to see Jackson. My heart has already done a small flip before I realize that no one is coming in. I sigh, disgusted at the mixture of hope and dread that makes me desperate to see him one minute and eager him to disappear in the next.

Constance must have noticed me looking towards the door. "Jackson's having dinner at the Gorman's," she tells me, and I wonder what else she's seen in my face. Her expression is bland, however, revealing nothing of her thoughts. "He hasn't been in Foster in a while, so he's been getting a lot of invitations."

I'll bet he has. I wonder if Lindsay is one of the people offering those invitations. "What about Lindsay?" I ask, my voice light and uninterested.

Constance studies my face for a moment. She knows what Lindsay did to me all those years ago, and I see uncertainty flit across her face before she replies. "She's recently divorced from Edgar Northgate," She tells me. I didn't even know Lindsay had married, but I knew of the ex-husband, a well-known multi-billionaire financier who must have been at least twice her age.

"She's back at the Gorman house," Constance continues, "although I have no idea why? Her divorce must have left her as rich as Soraya Khashoggi."

And now she's back in Foster, and Jackson is with her. I swallow the lump in my throat and turn to listen to something Nick is saying, willing myself to ignore the memories seeping into my mind and threatening to take me back to places I thought I'd left behind, and knowing that it's no use.

Chapter Eight

Past

ON my seventeenth birthday, Aunt Constance gives me an eReader, while Blythe sends me a lingerie set that's so revealing I'm actually embarrassed to look at it. *'For when you get lucky'* the accompanying note says. Ever since she started sleeping with Carter, she's been very outspoken on the joys of sex, and impatient for me to join her in what she calls the 'club of lovers' so we can have real adult conversations. I wish. I've barely seen Jackson since the day at the orchard. Last year he gave me a camera to replace my old one, this year, he hasn't even called or texted to say happy birthday, talk less of sending me a present.

Mrs. Shannon bakes me a delicious chocolate cake. Aunt Constance is in New York for the day, but she insists that I should have some friends over and have a party in the garden or by the pool. I don't have many friends. There's May, of course, and Chace, a bookish guy who became my friend after we shared a table in biology lab. He's as studious and nerdy as May is outgoing and bubbly. As soon as I tell her about the party, she takes over the planning, and by evening, we're having a very cool party by the pool.

"I heard some guy tried to sneak booze into your party and Mrs. Shannon caught him." I'm on the phone with Blythe, the day after my birthday.

"Yeah," I laugh. "She got the door, and somehow she knew, so she bumped into him and the bottle fell out of his jacket."

Blythe snorts with laughter.

"And then she caught it, it was like something out of Mr. and Mrs. Smith."

"I've always suspected she was ex-KGB," Blythe says, giggling, "or at least a vampire, only she doesn't glitter in the sun."

"A lot of vampires don't glitter in the sun," I laugh, "it totally depends on the type of moisturizer they use."

After a few more minutes spent laughing at vampire jokes, she has to go. It's hard, but I resist the temptation to ask her about Jackson in the hope that she would know why he has totally ignored my birthday.

I'm about to go back to enhancing a picture on my computer when, in the silence of the practically empty house, I hear the purr of a car engine coming up the drive. Aunt Constance is attending a dinner party at the Gorman's, and she won't be back until about midnight. I find myself hoping that it's Jackson on one of his unannounced visits to the house. I try to contain myself as I go downstairs, trying not to run down the stairs in my eagerness to see him. When the door opens and Jackson lets himself in, I'm already in the foyer, almost out of my mind with joy at the sight of him.

It never gets old, seeing him. The older we get, the more handsome, and irresistible he seems to become. Looking at him is as much agony as it is pleasure, but I can't tear my eyes away. He's like the sun, and I'm a helpless planet, revolving around him.

"Olivia."

I love that he still calls me that, ever since that first

time when he defied my mother's warning. Now it's like an intimate secret between us that he's the only person in the world who still calls me Olivia, It makes me feel so much closer to him.

"Hi Jackson," I say, doing my best to keep the breathless joy I've feeling out of my voice. "I didn't know you were coming home."

He frowns. "I... Yes... I was just in the area."

"Oh..." He probably came down with Lindsay to attend her parents' party. I decide, swallowing the feeling of disappointment. What did I expect? That he was here to see me?

He starts to walk towards me, and I forget my disappointment as I admire easy gracefulness with which he moves. He's perfect, and more than anything, I want to close the distance between us. I want to go to him, to put my arms around his waist, run my fingers through his hair...

"What are you still doing up?" he asks, when he reaches where I'm standing on the bottom stair.

I snap out of my less than innocent thoughts, and shrug, the careless movement belying the exquisite tension I'm feeling from standing so close to him. "I was working on a picture," I say, "and then I heard the car."

"Okay, picture-nerd." He laughs and put an arm around me, and I look up at him, blissful and wondering at the contact. He's looking down at me, his face so close to mine, that I'm sure he can feel the heat as my face flushes.

I freeze, my heart thumping in my chest, and my mouth suddenly dry. He doesn't move either. Our faces are so close that suddenly, I'm filled with a crazy hope that he would just lean further down, and kiss me.

Instead, his hand leaves my shoulder, and he moves away, going up the stairs and leaving me with no choice but to follow him. We're both silent, me torturing myself with wondering what he's thinking, and trying to understand the moment we had just had. At the top of the stairs, where the house split into the family wing and the guest wing, which is rarely used, he suddenly stops and turns around.

I stop too, hoping that he would say something to me, something to validate the wild hope in my chest that the moment we had at the bottom of the stairs, means something, not just to me, but also to him.

"Happy Birthday," He says, smiling apologetically, "I'm sorry I didn't call yesterday, but I got you something." He retrieves a box from his pocket.

I take it from him, hands shaking as I open it to

reveal a fine platinum chain with a heart shaped pendant. I reach for the pendant with trembling fingers, feeling the stones set in the metal, and the engraving of my name in flowing script.

"It's beautiful." I sigh, looking up at him. "Thank you Jackson."

He looks pleased that I like it. "You're welcome."

I don't know what comes over me at that moment, but when I smile at him, it's the most provocative and teasing smile I can manage. "Aren't you going to help me put it on?" I ask, taking my cue from all the movies and romance novels I've read over the years.

He gives me a quizzical look. "Okay." he says, after only a second's pause. He lifts the necklace out of the box, and I turn around, my body quivering as his fingers brush my neck.

When the necklace is fastened, I don't move. His fingers are still lightly touching my neck, but I'd rather die than break the contact.

At first, he doesn't move either, but after a moment, his fingers start to trace a slow path outward, from my neck to my shoulders.

I feel as if I'm floating. I can't breathe, and when I feel his lips touch my shoulder in a soft gentle kiss, a sigh escapes me.

I turn around, urged by his hands on my shoulders. When I look up at him, his eyes are fixed on my lips. I wait expectantly, my heart in my mouth, and my stomach twisted in excitement.

"Olivia." He says softly, looking up from my lips to meet my eyes. His eyes are smoldering, the fire in their depths echoing the one I feel raging in my body, and his voice is like a caress all over my skin.

"Jackson." My response is a soft whisper.

He makes a sound, a low groan, and then his lips are on mine, warm, tender, and lighting a fire in my stomach that heats my blood, my body, my soul.

He pulls me against him, and I moan with pleasure, pressing my body closer to him. I'm crushed against the hard muscles of his chest as his lips move softly over mine. It's the sweetest thing I've ever experienced. My heart is fluttering, and my stomach feels so light, I'm afraid it would float away.

I can't resist the urge to explore, and my fingers find their way into his hair, threading their way through the soft wavy mass. In response, he groans and deepens the kiss, his tongue delving into my mouth, caressing, tasting, and making my body sing.

Suddenly, he releases my lips, ending the kiss, but he doesn't pull away. He rests his forehead on mine, one hand still around my waist, and the other at the back of my neck, still holding me close to him. After a while, I open my eyes, and I see that he's smiling.

"Olivia." He draws out the sound of my name, still smiling, then he presses a kiss on both my cheeks, down on my collarbone, my shoulders, then back to my face, my eyes and my cheeks, each small kiss taking me further and further to the place where my heart will surely burst.

"You're perfect," he whispers between kisses.

I sigh, unable to keep standing without leaning on him for support. "Thanks," I whisper in reply, shyness and happiness, warring for supremacy in my head. One of my dreams had just come true. Jackson Lockewood has given me my first kiss, and it was perfect.

He chuckles softly as he runs a thumb over my lower lip, and then my cheek. "I wanted to do that for so long," He says, a small smile still on his lips. "You don't think I'm a shameless older guy taking advantage of you, do you?"

I shake my head. I can't find the words to tell him how I've longed for this, how my heart feels like it's going to rise right out of my chest and burst into a thousand shimmering stars. "You're not taking advantage of me," I say instead, "and anyway you're not much older than I am."

He seems to be thinking about what I said, but I don't want him to think, I want him to kiss me again. I'm too shy to say so, but somehow, as if he can read my mind, he lowers his lips to mine again, and this time, it's even better that the first time.

Somehow, we find our way to my room and end up on the bed. We don't do anything but kiss and talk. It's sweet and wonderful and beautiful all at the same time.

"Have you really wanted to kiss me for a long time?" I ask.

Jackson laughs and nuzzles my neck. "Amongst other things, Yes."

I giggle at the sensation of his nose against my throat. "So why didn't you?"

He is laying half on top of me on the bed. When I ask my question, he rests his weight on his elbows so he can look at me. His gaze is serious. "Had you ever been kissed before?"

I look away from his probing gray eyes, overwhelmed with shyness again. Slowly I shake my head.

"You're young, and inexperienced, and the decent thing to do…. That I've been trying to do, would be to let you have your high school adventures, your first crush, kiss, relationship, and all that with someone your own age." He's using his 'serious' voice, and I know he means every word he's saying, but he couldn't be more wrong.

"I've never wanted any of those things with anybody else, Jackson," I interrupt, making him stop talking. "It was always you."

Chapter Nine

Past

THE words hang in the air between us, and for a moment, Jackson does nothing other than look at me, his gray eyes, growing darker and stormier with each passing second. Suddenly, he's kissing me again, his body pressed against mine, so I can feel his hard chest against my breasts, and the unfamiliar tightness and bulge in his jeans pressing against my thigh. I want to be adventurous and touch him there, but I'm too much of a coward, and he seems perfectly satisfied to kiss me and kiss me until my whole body feels like I'm floating on a cloud of ecstasy.

After what I know only seems like a short while because I would gladly spend a lifetime kissing Jackson, I hear the sounds of another car coming up the drive.

"That's Aunt Constance." I say unnecessarily.

"I know." Jackson murmurs against my neck. He makes no move to get up, or to stop kissing me. We don't stop until we hear the sound of the front door opening and closing.

"She'll still be asleep when I leave tomorrow," Jackson tells me, "and there are a couple of things I need to talk to her about, or else I wouldn't leave you at all."

"You'll come back though, after you've spoken to her?"

He grins. "Try and stop me."

I follow him to the door and watch as he walks down the corridor. I still can't wrap my mind around the fact that he kissed me, that we've spent most of the evening kissing. I and Jackson! I want to whoop. I want to tell someone. I want to save the memory somewhere it will never be lost.

He stops at the top of the stairs, looks back at me, and winks. I can hear the sound of Aunt Constance's heels on the marble stairs. I should go back inside my room and wait for him. I'm already inside, about to close the door, when I hear her voice.

"Why did you leave so early?" She's saying to Jackson, "I looked for you for a bit before I realized you were gone, and Lindsay didn't look too happy either. Not very polite, if you ask me."

I'd already guessed that he came to town for the Gorman's party, but that had been before he kissed me. Sometime between then and now, I've convinced myself that he's really in Foster, at Halcyon, to see me. The disappointment I feel at having that hope dashed is raw and painful.

"I wasn't really in the mood for a party." I hear Jackson say through the haze of my hurt feelings. I don't want to hear any more, so I close the door, helpless against the anger, pain, and jealousy I'm feeling. I've just learned how much joy can come with being with someone you love, and now, just minutes later, I'm learning how much pain you can feel when they hurt you. Suddenly I feel raw and aching, unable to accept that Jackson came straight from his girlfriend's arms into mine. I can't bear it.

I toss the throw pillows off my bed in annoyance, working myself up to a state as I lie there, imagining Jackson and Lindsay together. I can't believe how happy I felt just a few moments ago and how angry and frustrated I feel now. By the time I hear the soft knock on my door followed by Jackson coming into my room, I've burned myself out. All I can feel is the agony of the realization that even though I've just being as intimate with him as I've never been with anyone else, he still isn't any more mine than he was before he kissed me.

I take one look at him, and the pain intensifies. I want to tell him how bad I feel, how angry I am that he came straight from his girlfriend to kiss me and make me feel as if I was special to him. But despite my outrage and the mess of emotions burning through me, I can't find the right words.

"Aunt Constance has gone to bed." He tells me, closing the door behind him.

I glare at him, confused by the mess of chaotic emotions I'm feeling. "Why did you kiss me when you're only in town to see your girlfriend?" I accuse.

He is only silent for a short moment. "She's not my girlfriend anymore," he says quietly as he walks towards the bed. His words fan a flame of hope in my belly, and I stare at him, unable to do anything other than hope that he's saying what I think he's saying.

"What happened?" I ask.

He shrugs. "Nothing," he says, coming to sit beside me on the bed. "She saw your necklace in my pocket and she lost it." He shrugs, "She had a lot of nasty things to say about you, about me."

"Like what."

"It doesn't matter." He pauses, "Anyway we broke up."

I try to look sad, to mourn the end of a relationship, but I really can't, not when it's what I've wanted for far too long. "I'm sorry." I lie.

"I'm not," He smiles at me. "It was bound to happen sooner or later."

I don't argue with him, not when my heart is singing. I sit up and reach for his face, kissing him, and sighing against his lips when they start to move over mine, caressing them and probing them apart. I moan when his tongue finds mine, tasting and teasing me, while his hands map a sweet, gentle path across my body.

I reach inside his shirt, forgetting my shyness as my fingers explore the hard muscles of his stomach and chest. I run my finger over a nipple, and he sighs, his body trembling a little.

"You're shaking." I tell him, surprised that my touch can affect him so much.

He chuckles, stroking my face as he looks at me. "I've had you inside my head for what seems like forever, like a fever that never goes away." There's something vulnerable about his face as he looks intently at me. "And now I don't want any part of this to end... do you understand?"

I nod, my feelings alternating between joy and absolute bliss. "I've wanted this too." I say, "From the first time I saw you."

He laughs. "You were fourteen."

I chuckle. "And you were beautiful."

He pulls me close and kisses me some more, and as

my body melts into his, I know that those kisses will not be enough. I want to be a part of him. I want to belong to him totally. So when his hand moves up along my belly, and comes to a stop right before it reaches my breast, I look into his face. "Don't stop." I whisper. "Please."

He doesn't need any urging. He cups my breasts in his palms and I feel them swell and strain against the restraint of my clothes, aching for the fulfillment I've imagined a thousand times but never felt. I lose myself to his touch, moaning as his fingers find my swollen nipples and tease them through my clothes.

When my hands drift down for my fingers to stroke the hardness in his trousers, he groans, giving me a heady feeling of power.

"Don't do that," he warns.

"Why not?" I ask, afraid of doing anything to spoil the moment.

"I won't be able to stop."

"I don't want you to stop." I tell him earnestly.

He is silent, but only for a moment, before leans down and kisses me again. This time his kiss is determined, insistent. I melt into it, reveling in each touch of his lips as they travel down from my lips, over my still clothed breasts to my stomach. A soft moan escapes me when he lifts my top and drops kisses on my bare belly. He pulls my top over my head, and soon my bra follows, and then his lips are on my breasts, kissing me all around the tender aching flesh before taking my nipple into his mouth and gently sucking on it.

I almost vault off the bed at the exquisite pleasure. I don't feel like myself anymore, especially when he gently shushes me and continues licking my breasts. I feel as if I'm going mad, as if my body has become something else, an unfamiliar mass of new and incredible sensations. Just when I feel like I might explode, he abandons one erect nipple for the other, giving it the same attentions, until I know my body is going to explode.

While his lips are busy at my breasts, he undoes the waistband of my jeans, and his fingers slide in to stroke me gently through my panties, moving in slow circular motions.

"Olivia." he groans, his face drawn into a tortured frown. He takes my lips again, his fingers still stroking me through my panties. I start to move my hips to their rhythm, intent on prolonging the sensations his fingers are creating.

"Jackson." I moan questioningly, as I start to lose control of my body.

"Relax," he urges softly, without pausing in what he's doing.

I feel my body loosening and becoming fluid, then it tightens and arches of the bed as unbearable pleasure fills me. I scream, but immediately Jackson's lips are on mine, swallowing the sound, his fingers keeping on their movement until I fall back on the bed with a sigh.

His lips find my nipples again, swollen with the aftermath of the most incredibly pleasurable experience ever, and when he starts to suck on them, my body spirals towards mindless pleasure again.

I reach for his shirt and pull it off, exposing his firmly muscled chest. When I reach for his pants, his hand covers mine. "Olivia."

"Please." my voice is soft and imploring. I want this badly. I don't think I'll feel complete until I can give him the kind of pleasure he's just given me. I want him to lose himself as I just lost myself, and I want it to be because of me.

Gently, he pushes my fingers away and undoes his belt. I watch, mesmerized as he pulls off his pants, exposing the hard ridge of his erection straining against his briefs. I only feel uncertainty for a second, before I lean forward and kiss his chest, his nipples, getting a moan from him. He reaches for my jeans and pulls them off. My panties follow, and then his briefs.

He kisses me again, long and hard. "Are you sure?" he asks.

In reply, I reach for him, trembling as my fingers touch the smooth skin stretched taut over his hard length, like velvet over steel. I encircle him with my fingers and stroke up and down the full length. He trembles visibly, his eyes closed as a sigh escapes his lips.

He pushes me back on the bed, his fingers reaching between my legs to stroke the sensitive wetness there. I moan softly, my legs spreading wider, giving him space to kneel between them, his erection poised to enter me.

I wait impatiently as he reaches for his discarded trousers and extracts his wallet from the pocket. I know what he's doing even before I hear the sound of the foil tearing. I don't want to imagine why he carries a condom in his wallet or think of all the other girls he's been with. I reach for him and pull him closer, gasping as his tip presses against me, moving slowly, but firmly inside me.

I stiffen at the pain, trying my best not to cry out, but unable to prevent the sting of tears in my ears.

"Shhh." Jackson whispers, kissing my eyes. "I'm sorry."

"I'm fine." I tell him. I'm not lying. As the initial pain fades, it's replaced by a growing and insistent need. My hips clench involuntarily, wanting something more, and I feel Jackson stiffen, a small moan escaping his lips. Then he moves, stroking my insides in a surprisingly pleasurable movement that I feel to the tip of my fingers. When I moan my pleasure, he continues, moving in and out of me as my body clenches around him. I cry out, my fingers gripping the sheets, Jackson's shoulders, his hair, as intense pleasure takes over my body. My hips are moving to match his rhythm, milking the sensations. I feel the warm pulsing pleasure build between my legs, taking over me until my whole body tightens, and I cry out my release in a long helpless moan. Jackson's arms tighten around me as he plunges deep into me, his body stiffening as he comes.

"Are you okay?" he asks later, as he pulls me into his arms.

I only smile, because I have no words to describe how he's made me feel, how, in that moment, I feel as if I'm the only girl in the world, and all my dreams have come true.

Chapter Ten

Past

JACKSON leaves early the next morning, but not even that can dampen my happiness. I feel like a different person, like it's a different world. Being in love and knowing that the object of my affection feels the same way is like floating on a cloud. Nothing can bring me down.

He comes home as often as he can manage, but it's not enough. I want to see him every day, to feel the beauty of surrendering my body to him as often as I can.

We don't tell anyone about us, at first Jackson wants

to, but even though I don't really think that Aunt Constance will disapprove of us, I want to wait, at least until I go to college, and we no longer live in the same house. I'm planning to go to college in New York in the fall, and since he's going to be in the city too, taking a position at some investment management firm, we'll be close, and then we can tell everyone that we're together.

"Honey, could you ask Blythe if Jackson's told her when he'll be back?" Aunt Constance looks up from the sheet of paper she's studying on the desk. We're in the study, and she's going over the menu for Jackson's graduation party for like the hundredth time. Even though she's been up all day planning the party, she still looks flawless, her hair held up in a small French knot, and her clothes smooth and perfect. Trying to look as good as she does all the time is as daunting for me as it's effortless for her. Sometimes I believe that she would look perfect and put together even in a storm.

"I'll ask," I reply, leaving the study to find Blythe, and thinking that perhaps I should just call and ask Jackson myself. Carter is with Blythe by the pool, and they've been making out and God-knows-what-else all afternoon. She's totally useless to anyone else when Carter is around, not that I blame her, not when I know what it feels like to be with the person you love.

Outside on the patio, the day is sunny and bright, and on the far side of the lawn across from the pool, I can see

UNDENIABLE

the workmen still setting up the buffet tables. I make my way to the pool, and as I already knew, Blythe and Carter, are lying on one of the loungers, kissing enthusiastically.

I want to say 'get a room,' and I know they probably will. For a second, I allow myself to wonder what it would feel like not to care who knew that I was in love with Jackson, to be able to kiss him and touch him anywhere and at any time. I can't help feeling a little jealous.

"Hey," I call out.

They ignore me of course, too intent on sucking each other's faces.

"Hey Blythe," I say a little louder.

Blythe finally pulls her mouth from Carter's and turns to face me. I pretend not to see Carter pulling his hand out of the waistband of her shorts. She looks hot, sweaty, and in need of a dip in the pool, or a cold shower, or both.

"Nice timing Livvie," She says with a sigh.

"Hi Livvie." Carter echoes with a smirk in my direction.

"Hi Carter." I reply, resisting the urge to respond to his smirk with a frown. It's easy to see why Blythe likes him. He's incredibly handsome, with the kind of good looks that are so perfect that it's sometimes hard to look at him and not gawk. Aunt Constance does not approve of him, and her reservations have driven a small wedge

107

between her and Blythe. I'm not exactly sure, but I think Aunt Constance's disapproval may have something to do with the blank look that never quite leaves Carter's face these days, and the way his eyes sometimes burn brightly when he comes out of the bathroom. I don't know all the signs of drug addiction, but I'm sure Aunt Constance suspects him of being an addict.

"Aunt Constance wants to know if Jackson's told you when he'll get home," I tell Blythe. Jackson is driving down from Boston, and Aunt Constance is concerned that he should have time to rest before the party.

"No," Blythe frowns, "Is she worried? I'm sure he'll turn up. Jackson wouldn't miss his own party."

"Why don't you call him?" Carter says, winking at me as he strokes his fingers slowly up and down Blythe's arm.

She turns back to him, and they start to kiss again. I realize I've been dismissed, and go back into the house, frowning as I realize that Carter's stepsister, Jackson's ex Lindsay will probably be here tonight.

The last time I saw her in town, she took one look at the necklace Jackson gave me for my last birthday and gave me a glare that was scornful and chilling at the same time. I know she's aware that Jackson gave it to me. They had a fight about it, right before he broke up with her.

Well I'm not worried about her. I doubt that she knows about Jackson and me, and even if she blames me or my treasured necklace for their breakup, there's nothing she can do about it.

"I can't get through to him." Aunt Constance frets when I tell her what Blythe said. "I just hope I'm planning the right kind of party for college students... and grads. I keep thinking they'd rather all go to a club." She sighs. "Did you buy a dress?"

"Yes." I say excitedly. She'd given me a gift card and an appointment at one of her favorite stores so I could get a dress for the party. It wasn't that I couldn't afford to buy a good dress on my own, but an appointment with one of the shoppers at Aunt Constance's favorite shops is like fashion gold, and a step closer to looking as effortlessly perfect as she always does.

"Well enjoy yourself tonight, and don't do anything I wouldn't approve of." She gives me a cautioning smile,

"Blythe will take care of me." I say half-jokingly. "Don't worry."

She snorts. "If she can keep her hands off that boy for long enough." A cloud comes over her face, but it's only for a moment. "Why don't you go rest?" She tells me. "I can manage from here."

I leave her in the study and go upstairs to my room, already inside before I realize I'm not alone. I feel the familiar shiver of anticipation going down my spine, and even before I look towards the bed and see Jackson sitting on it, I already know it's him.

He's wearing a dark blue shirt, jeans, and a wide grin,

looking slightly disheveled but sexy as hell.

"Jackson!" I exclaim.

He puts a finger to his lips. "Shhh, come here."

I go to him eagerly, sighing as he pulls me onto his lap and starts to kiss me.

"I was downstairs and I didn't hear your car." I say, when I come up for breath.

"I didn't drive." He lies back on the bed. "I was at a party last night, and I caught a ride home with Shane Colton," he grins, "He doesn't drink."

Shane Colton lives miles away towards the edge of the town. "So you walked all the way from the Colton's." I ask, incredulous.

"Along the river," he tells me with a shrug. "How's it going downstairs? I saw the tables on the lawn."

"Aunt Constance is wondering when you'll arrive." I say.

He chuckles. "I wouldn't miss my own party." He runs a finger along my cheek. "How're you doing?"

I shrug. "Okay."

"I've missed you." He says, pulling me closer and kissing me again.

My body lights up. I've missed this, missed him so much. I reach for him, pulling at his clothes, and helping him get rid of mine, my frantic desire for him growing as his hands set fire to my skin and my blood. We've done this so many times now, but each time it still feels new and different. When we're naked, I reach for him, sighing as my fingers close around him. He's still sitting on the bed, and I slide down, so I'm kneeling in front of him. He groans when I take him in my mouth, his hands fisting in my hair as he throws his head back.

I suck on him, flicking my tongue around the silken skin and watching the muscles of his chest tighten as he tries to hold on to his control. With an impatient sound, he reaches for me, pulling me up, so I'm straddling him. I wait impatiently while he rolls on a condom, and then takes hold of my hips, lowering me unto his long hard length. I groan, moving my hips so I can feel every single inch of him inside me.

His hands tighten on my hips as he starts to thrust into me, holding me steady as he drives my body insane. In only a few moments, I start to shake, moaning incoherently, my body quivering as I come apart around him and fall unto his chest.

He's not done, still hard, he rolls over without letting go of me, so that I'm lying on my back, and he's on top of me, then he starts to thrust again. Pleasure takes over me, and I'm sure the whole house can hear my moans. I don't even know when I wrap my legs around his waist, urging him deeper. He groans and starts to move faster, each stroke taking me higher and higher until I can't bear it anymore. I hear his loud groan as he slams into me one last time and comes, the same moment as my body tightens and explodes.

Afterwards, we lie there naked and kissing. I love being so close to him, feeling the warmth of his body around me.

"I've missed you." I say.

"Me too," He kisses my forehead.

"Where's Blythy?" he asks after a while.

"Out by the pool with Carter," I tell him.

His expression hardens, but it's only for a fleeting moment. "I'm going to go down to see Aunt Constance," he says, getting up from the bed and putting on his clothes. When he's done, he gives me a light kiss on my lips. "See you at the party." He says.

I nod, admiring his perfect body as he walks to the door and leaves the room. It won't be long now, I think happily, before we can really be together.

I'm about to doze off when I notice that, on the nightstand beside my bed, the light on my phone is blinking. I read the text from May.

So excited, cant wait tanx for inviting me to hang with yummy Jackson, and his yummy friends.

I sigh. May is such a boy freak, but it's part of her charm. She doesn't have a boyfriend because her ideal man, according to her, only exists between the covers of her billionaire romance novels.

There's another text, but it's from Chace.

May drove by my house. I swear she's hyperventilating about meeting hot guys, tempted to sedate her so she wakes up tomorrow after the party. See you at seven.

I smile, wondering if Chace and May would even be friends if not for me. Her bubbly nature amuses him, and his insistence on hiding his cuteness behind his glasses and the nerd hair confuses her. I invited them both to Jackson's party, and I'm sure we'll have fun watching people get drunk.

It's only two hours until the party starts. Soon Blythe would burst into my room, frantically asking which one of several dresses I think she should wear instead of the one she's chosen before. Aunt Constance would leave for the quiet dinner she's having at a friend's so as not to be in the way, and then the guests would fill the house. It will be fun, but I'm more excited about Jackson, and after the party, when it will be just the two of us again, talking about our future, and making love until we're exhausted.

May is mouthing the words to poker face and channeling Lady Gaga on the terrace, which is the dance floor for tonight. Chace and I are seated on the steps at the edge of the terrace, watching her, and taking pictures on our phones to torment her with later. There are other people on the dance floor, but nobody is dancing like May is dancing.

My eyes follow Jackson as he chats with his friends and dances with a couple of girls. We danced too at some point, his hand around my waist would have seemed innocent to onlookers, but I knew what the look in his eyes meant, and it made me eager and impatient for the party to be over.

I never get tired of looking at him, and sometimes it's hard to believe that he's mine, this guy who most of the girls in the room would give a hand to go out with. As if he can hear my thoughts, he turns to look at me and as our eyes meet. He grins at me, and I smile back.

"One day you'll tell me what's going on with you guys." Chace says.

"Who says anything is going on?" I retort, without looking away from Jackson.

Chace shakes his head, making his curly hair bounce over his glasses. "I'm not blind."

"But you're imagining things."

He yawns. "My imagination is busy with important stuff, but I can't help that I can see the calf love right in front of me."

"Calf what...!" I smack him playfully on his arm. "Anyway, it's not like you would know, you don't know anything about any kind of love."

He shrugs and adjusts his glasses. "May's going to hate herself tomorrow if she spends the whole night dancing like a ninja."

We both laugh, still laughing when someone trips over my feet and spills her drink on my new dress.

"I'm so sorry." She exclaims, baby blue eyes so sincerely apologetic that I immediately suspect that it's an act. It's Lindsay Gorman, Jackson's ex.

"It's okay." I tell her resignedly.

She smiles and walks on. "Now I have to change." I complain to Chace."

He shrugs. "Or you could just pretend that the wet patch is part of the design."

"Thanks Chace." I roll my eyes. "I'll be right back."

He nods and goes back to watching May. I walk into the deserted house and make my way upstairs to my room. It's dark inside except for the dim light from the window. Reaching for the light switch, I'm about to flip them on when strong arms pull me towards a rock hard chest.

I only manage to wonder how Jackson got upstairs so fast before lips descend on mine, hard, forceful, and smelling of alcohol. That's when I realize that it's not Jackson. Someone else is in my room. Someone else is kissing me, and my arms are locked so tightly to his chest I can't even struggle.

He moves, pushing me against the wall and crushing me with his body until my back hurts. Terror rises like bile in my throat. I try to scream, but his tongue is in my mouth, and I can make nothing more than a few muffled sounds.

Cold fear grips me when I hear the sound of my zipper tearing as he rips my dress down from the neckline, taking my strapless bra with it. I push against him, desperation filling me as I realize I'm no match for his strength. I'm still trying ineffectually to free myself when his hand covers my breasts, squeezing them roughly.

Please, I plead silently, please whoever you are, don't do this.

Suddenly the lights come on, and the weight pressing me against the wall is gone. I open my eyes, lightheaded with the aftermath of panic, and the relief at being free of my attacker, and I see Carter standing in front of me, wiping my lipstick from his lips.

I stare at him, speechless. For a moment, I can't even think clearly.

Did Carter just try to rape me?

He looks repentant, panicked even. He's looking towards the door. Realizing that someone else must have put on the lights, I follow Carter's gaze and see Blythe at the door, a look of disbelief, shock, and anger on her face.

"What the hell?" she cries, the words ending in a sob.

"Blythe I'm sorry." Carter says, "She just jumped me."

It takes a moment for me to process his words. I stare at him in disbelief. "What?"

"How could you?" Blythe screams at me. "I saw you, you were kissing him."

"Blythe he was…"

"Don't say my name." She cries. "Don't even say my name."

Suddenly I feel weak, unable to support my own weight. I lean against the wall, shaking, only managing to pull up my dress to cover my breasts, before footsteps announce that someone else has arrived.

I look up and see Jackson behind Blythe at the door.

"Lindsay thought she heard shouting upstairs," he says, moving past Blythe to come into the room. He takes one look at me, and he's immediately at my side. "What happened?" He asks, his hand on my shoulder, "Are you all right?" He turns to Carter, and in the next moment, he shoves Carter so hard, Carter stumbles and almost falls.

"What the fuck happened?" he barks.

"Leave him alone." Blythe cries, rushing to Carter's side.

Jackson turns back to me. His hands are on my shoulders again, his eyes full of concern. "Tell me what happened."

Blythe turns a fiery look at her brother. "Livvie was kissing Carter is what happened." She spits, glaring at me with an expression that's close to hatred. "She was practically naked, and her hands were all over him."

The words seem to freeze the air, or maybe its

Jackson's eyes, as they suddenly turn to ice. His hands tighten on my shoulders, and then they're gone, suddenly, as if the touch of my skin has stung him.

"I'm sorry." I hear Carter say to Blythe. "I was up on the corridor looking for you, and she came up and said her zipper was stuck, and then she was all over me."

By now Jackson's eyes are positively glacial, and the way he's looking at me, as if he doesn't know me, as if we haven't spent the last few months getting to know each other in the most intimate possible ways, as if I'm the liar, the slut Carter and Blythe are accusing me of being.

A part of me is still convinced that he would wait, allow me to tell him the truth. That part dies when he turns and roughly shoves Carter out of the way, before walking out of the room. He's followed by Blythe, who's pulling on Carter's hand, while he follows her, his head bowed in an expression of perfect contrition.

I spend the night in my room, not even bothering to say goodbye to my friends. At first all I can do is throw up, retching until my stomach feels like a raw aching mess. I keep seeing the look on Jackson's face, anger, and even disgust. I can't believe that he and Blythe both choose to believe Carter without even asking me what happened.

'Carter Felton is one of them,' a voice in my head whispers, *'you're only a charity case, why would they even care anything about you?'*

I don't want to believe that my thoughts are right, but if Blythe were my friend, wouldn't she have asked me what happened? If Jackson loved me, wouldn't he have waited for me to defend myself before judging me?

'He was only using you.' The hateful inner voice continues, and it goes on like that all night. By morning, my eyes are red from crying, and I'm heartsick from waiting for Jackson to come to my room and ask for my side of the story.

When I venture downstairs, the house is silent. Luckily, I don't see anyone on the way downstairs. I don't think I can face Blythe, or even Jackson. I just want to tell Aunt Constance everything, because I know she'll at least listen to me.

I hear her voice through the door to the study before I enter. She's talking on the phone, and when she notices me, she frowns and holds up a hand to tell me to wait for her to finish her conversation. I stand there nervous and waiting, the knot in my stomach growing until I feel as if I might start to throw up again.

Finally, when she's done, she turns to me. "What were you thinking?" she starts. She looks stern, and her voice sounds impatient and almost annoyed. "You ruined the party for the both of them. Blythe's left town and God knows where Jackson is. I haven't seen or heard from him since last night."

With each word that comes out of her mouth, my misery increases, somehow I'd thought that even if everyone else believed Carter over me, she wouldn't. She was my last hope that somewhere in this house, there was someone who would give me a chance. I close my eyes against the tears and desperation threatening to come to the surface. Suddenly I want my mom and my dad. They would have listened to me. They would have believed me, and they would have made sure Carter paid for what he tried to do to me.

Aunt Constance mistakes my silence for remorse. She sighs sympathetically. "Olivia, I understand that at your age making out with a cute guy can seem like it's the most important thing in the world, but there are other things that matter, like loyalty to people who have been kind to you."

I swallow the painful lump in my throat. I can't even look at her. I've spent so long admiring her and wanting to emulate her, and I can't reconcile those feelings to the sense of anger and betrayal I feel towards her right now.

I want to throw a tantrum, to scream, to demand that she asks me what really happened, but I decide that it's no use. She has judged me, concluded about me, even before hearing me out. She's picked Blythe and Carter over me, as she always will.

"You'll have to apologize to Blythe," she pronounces, dismissing me. "Heaven knows she's crazy enough about that boy to never want to see your face again."

With that, she turns away and goes back to whatever she was working on. My eyes are smarting as I leave the study and walk out of the house. Outside, the sky is so blue and the day so beautiful that it makes no sense how miserable I feel. The tables on the lawn are gone. The whole place is as spotless as if the party never happened. I wish it had never happened. I wish I could erase yesterday from my memory, and everyone else's too.

I walk down the drive, past the gates, and out onto the road, and I keep on walking for what seems like hours until I get to the cemetery.

It's a peaceful place. The silence only disturbed by the rustling of leaves on the trees along the perimeter, which shield the graves from the street. There's no gate, so I just walk in through the paved drive, passing old graves and new ones, simple headstones and elaborate ones until I get to the spot where my parents are buried.

I remove the carcasses of the flowers I left the last time I was there. In my misery, I'd forgotten to bring new ones, so there's nothing to replace them.

Leaning against the headstone, a thick, black, slab of granite, I trace my fingers over the engravings of my parents' names, the dates of their births and deaths, as well as the words, *'Loving Parents.'* Near the bottom of the headstone, the phrase "To live in the hearts of those you love is not to die," is engraved in script. I requested those words to be added, but now I know they mean nothing. When you die, you're gone, and you leave the ones you love behind, and no matter how long they keep you in their hearts you never come back to help them when they need you the most.

I start to cry, depressed with the unfairness of everything. For the first time in a long time, I find myself wishing we'd never moved to Foster. Maybe then I wouldn't be so miserable. Maybe my parents would still be alive, maybe I'd never have met Jackson, and he'd never have broken my heart.

As if I'm not miserable enough, it's starts to rain. It's only a small drizzle, but it's enough to make me feel as if the whole universe has conspired against me. I leave the grave and start the walk back to Halcyon, imagining how the whole of Foster must have heard by now that I tried to steal Blythe Lockewood's boyfriend, even Chace and May would have heard some version. Would they judge me too, believe what everyone is saying without giving me the benefit of the doubt? The thought makes me even sadder. I wish I didn't have to face anyone ever again. I wish I could float away in the air or something, and let go of my misery as I go.

By the time I get back to the house, Jackson's car is parked in the drive. It wasn't there when I left, and my heart tightens with apprehension at the thought of facing him. Instead of going into the house, I turn towards the gardens, picking my way through the flowers and shrubs to the lily pond and the gazebo that overlooks it. Somewhere in my mind is the thought of remaining there until I can sneak into the house without the risk of running into Jackson and facing his condemnation again.

The lilies are blooming in the pond, and they look beautiful as they float on the surface of the water. I stare at them for a while before I go towards the gazebo. It's a small structure with a tiled roof, round, with chest high walls topped with well-tended flower boxes. I used to come here to be alone when I first started living with the Lockewoods, and right now, I need the solace I always found here.

I climb the two steps into the small space, and freeze when I see Jackson lying inside, his long frame taking up at least four of the seats that line the walls. He's facing towards the ceiling, his eyes closed, and as I stand there frozen, unsure whether to walk in or go back, he turns towards me.

His eyes are cold, looking through me, almost as if he doesn't recognize me. From his expression, I may well be a piece of furniture, or some rubbish the wind blew in to disturb his solitude.

I can't bear his contempt. On one hand, I want to go in and explain what really happened last night, but what if he doesn't believe me, what if he calls me a liar.

I start to turn around, suddenly eager to leave, to escape the accusation in his silence, but as I start to move, he springs up from his lying position.

"Olivia."

Just my name, but it starts such a torrent of emotions inside me. I pause, waiting for him to say something, to ask me what really happened, but he doesn't. He just keeps looking at me, his face impassive, leaving me to wonder what he's thinking.

I take a step inside the small space. "Jackson..." I begin.

He doesn't let me finish. He moves fast, reaching me in only two quick strides, and suddenly his fingers are lacing through my hair, lifting my face up to his as he crushes my lips with his.

There's no gentleness in his kiss. It's deep and demanding, but all I can feel is relief and happiness to be so close to him again.

He wouldn't kiss me like this if he didn't think Carter was lying, I think blissfully, as I surrender myself to him. His tongue pushes into my mouth, stroking mine, while his free hand grips my waist, pressing my body against his. I kiss him back, reveling in the feel of his chest against my breasts, desperate to show him that it's him that I want. Just him, and no one else.

Without breaking the kiss, he moves his hands to my

breasts, squeezing them both as he runs a thumb over my swollen nipples. A moan escapes me, as I lose myself in pleasure.

Suddenly, he pulls his lips from mine. I look up into his face, wondering why he's stopped. His breathing is heavy and ragged, and his eyes are unfocused with arousal. He wants me, I think jubilantly, nothing has changed between us.

"What were you playing at?" His voice is like cold water on my skin. "Wasn't it enough to have one guy crazy over you, you had to go for Carter too? Was it just him, Olivia? How many more were there?"

I close my eyes, tears welling up as pain rises like a flood through my veins. "Jackson..."

He's not listening. He lowers his head and takes my lips again, mercilessly burying all my desperate explanations beneath the pleasurable assault of his lips. I find myself getting lost in what he is doing. Somewhere inside, I'm afraid that if I try to explain, that he'll stop, and I don't want that.

He pulls me further into the gazebo, towards the seats, taking off my blouse and unhooking my bra, impatiently tossing them on the floor before he takes possession of my breasts with his lips and his hands. I cry out in pleasure, surrendering the insane pleasurable pulsing between my legs, and unwilling to acknowledge the dark cloud hanging over everything we're doing.

His lips move up from my breasts over my collarbone, licking a trail of pleasure back to my lips, gently pushing me unto the seats while he works open the button of my jeans, his hand slipping inside to stroke me through my panties, making my body convulse.

"Oh Jackson," I moan against his lips, writhing against his hand, and feeling my body tighten as pleasure builds up. When I'm almost certain that I'm going to explode, he stops stroking me, leaving me in desperate need for him.

I wait impatiently as he pulls down my jeans, and then his mouth is on me, his lips nuzzling me and sending tingles all over my body. His tongue strokes between my folds, and it's warm and oh so sweet. He licks me until I'm blind, deaf, and screaming with helpless pleasure.

Then he turns me around, bending me over the seats, and spreading my legs with his knee. I wait impatiently while he undoes his trousers, and before long, I can feel his arousal probing me from behind, and slowly pushing inside to fill me completely.

I moan and grip the edge of the seat, feeling pleasure suffuse my body from my head to my toes. Almost immediately he's moving, sliding smoothly in and out of me, each stroke so unbelievably sweet that I can almost feel myself going insane. His hands are around my breasts, gripping and squeezing as he thrusts into me from behind. My whole body fills with heat. It spreads from between my legs until it consumes me, until I lose control, my nails digging into the fabric of the seats as I surrender to my climax.

His fingers continue to tease my nipples, as he keeps moving, prolonging my pleasure. It feels so good that I can feel the heat and the pleasure building up again. Waves upon waves of ecstasy washing over me as Jackson stiffens and slams into me one last time, groaning as he comes inside me.

I collapse on the seat, trying to catch my breath. Jackson pulls out of me, the movement sending aftershocks of pleasure flowing through me. He gets up, and immediately starts to adjust his clothes.

I lie there, half-naked, and feeling exposed, wondering what I should say, somehow knowing from the way he doesn't look at me, that he's rejecting me and what we just did.

"Jackson…" I venture, wanting at least to tell him how I feel, how desperate I am for him, how impossible it would be even for me to be remotely attracted to anyone else. Surely, he has to believe me. He has to know that he owns me, totally, completely.

He looks at me, and the expression I see in his face almost kills me. He looks angry and sad, with such an expression of self-loathing. I don't want to believe that he feels that way because of what's happened between us. I get up and start to put on my clothes. He's fully dressed before I am, and he watches me pull up my jeans his face, almost like a stranger's.

I pick up my panties and put them my pocket, embarrassed, nervous, afraid, and hopeful. I'm such a jumble of confused emotions. I want him to tell me that I have somehow misunderstood, that he knows Carter was lying about what happened.

But he doesn't say anything, and his expression doesn't change from the look of slight disgust, whether at himself for still wanting me, or at me for being the slut that he thinks I am, I don't know.

I watch as he turns and walks away, leaving me standing there alone.

I start to cry, thinking how differently I'd expected last night to end, where I'd thought our relationship was going, and I feel like a fool. I stay in the gazebo as long as I can. When I get back into the house, its silent, and Jackson's car is not in the driveway. I don't need anyone to tell me that he has gone.

Chapter Eleven

Past

SOMEHOW, I manage to get through the next few weeks. It's awful. In school, someone has spread the rumor that I tried to steal Blythe Lockewood's boyfriend. Suddenly, I'm a slut, and where before, I've only ever been an object of mild curiosity as the girl who lives in the Lockewood mansion, now I'm a recipient of open scorn.

I spend most of my time studying, and sometimes taking pictures, using the camera Jackson gave me, even though each time, it reminds me of him, and with the memories come the unavoidable pain. I haven't seen or heard from him since that day at the gazebo. He lives and works in the city now, and I'm sure all our plans to be together when I move to the city in the fall now mean nothing to him.

I haven't seen Blythe either, and now I'm sure Aunt Constance was right when she said Blythe would never want to see my face again. Even Aunt Constance has been spending more time working away from the house, giving me a dreadful feeling of being shut out, unwanted, and sad... so incredibly sad.

If not for Chace and May, I'd have gone mad the last few weeks of high school, but they were there for me, but not anymore, Chace is spending the summer in New York, taking early college classes at Columbia, and May is vacationing in Spain with her family.

I hear the sound of a car from the house, and I straighten, leaving my camera to rest on my chest, hanging from the rope around my neck. The bird I'd been trying to capture chirps and flies up to land on a branch overhead. It's late afternoon and around the gazebo and the lily pond, the shadows are already lengthening, adding a tranquil beauty to the scene.

Aunt Constance must have come back home. Ever since that night of Jackson's graduation party, our relationship has lost the closeness it once had. She hasn't changed, but I have. I can't stop thinking about the fact that she never trusted me enough to ask me what really happened.

After a while, I start back towards the house. I don't expect to see anyone when I go in, but I see Aunt Constance going up the grand staircase, phone held to her ear. She sees me at the door and waves, beckoning me to come up with her.

I follow her up the stairs, walking behind her while half-listening to her side of the conversation on the phone. In her bedroom, I go to stand by the window and look outside. I can see the gardens and the trees that border it, and through the trees, glimpses of the lily pond and the gazebo. I blush when I realize that if she'd been here that morning, she could have seen Jackson and me.

Jackson.

Even the thought of his name makes me want to cry.

"Jackson will be home for dinner tonight." Aunt Constance says, unknowingly torturing me further. "He called and said he'll be in town, but just for tonight, and he's coming with a friend."

My throat catches as I wrestle with the surge of hope and despair that comes when I think of seeing him. Will he listen to me now? Is he coming to see me, or did I not even factor in his decision to come home?

"Are you all right Livvie? You look a little pale." Aunt Constance frowns as she studies me.

"I'm fine," I tell her, even though I'm actually feeling

not only tired, but also extremely depressed. I want to lie down and wake up when I've forgotten everything that happened with Jackson and Carter and Blythe.

She tilts her head as she studies me. "Maybe you should see a doctor," She says, more to herself than to me. "I'll arrange it tomorrow, okay." She settles on the couch by the window and pats the space next to her, inviting me to sit too. "I spoke with Blythe today." She says softly. "It appears that Carter has been arrested."

Did he try to rape someone else, I wonder, surprised by the amount of satisfaction I feel at the news. I never liked Carter, but now, I dislike him so much I have to resist the urge to throw up whenever I think of him and what he almost did to me.

Aunt Constance is looking at me, waiting for me to say something. When I don't, she continues.

"He broke down and confessed a lot of things to Blythe. Apparently, he's been doing drugs for a while. His parents found out and cut him off when he refused to go to rehab, but his sister has been funding his habit."

"Lindsay?"

"Yes." Aunt Constance sighs. "What did you do to her? It appears that she'd convinced Carter that you wanted him to sleep with him." She looks uncomfortable, "She told him to wait for you in your room that night, and told him that it was your idea."

I remember Carter's smirks and winks, the way his

eyes had often lingered on me as if we shared a secret. "Then she spilled her drink on my dress so I would go up to my room."

Aunt Constance nods. "Blythe says Lindsay told her you needed her to help pick out another dress."

Then she told Jackson she's heard shouting upstairs, I remember, because it hadn't been my friendship with Blythe that she'd wanted to ruin, but my relationship with Jackson.

"Carter was high, and he says he got carried away, and he doesn't remember what happened, but when he saw Blythe he got scared and blamed it on you."

He doesn't remember. A bitter laugh hovers on my lips, almost escaping. He doesn't remember, and I haven't been able to forget.

"Did he hurt you?" Aunt Constance asks. She looks scared, as if the thought that something bad could have happened to me while in her care would be a failure on her part. I debate what to tell her. That he pushed me against the wall, ripped off the top of my dress? I don't even want to remember it.

"Not that much." I say. "Blythe came before anything happened."

Aunt Constance releases a long breath. "But why would Lindsay do something like that?" She muses.

I took Jackson from her, I say silently. She blamed me for breaking them up, enough to want to turn everyone I cared about against me.

Aunt Constance is still waiting for me to reply. "Nothing," I reply. "I don't even know her that well."

"I assume she may have been jealous about how close you are to Blythe, or maybe something else." She sighs. "Teenage girls can be very vindictive." She looks at me. "Blythe is pretty torn up. She says she was so angry she forgot to wonder why Lindsay had sent her up to your room in the first place. She says she's sorry, but she's going to have to tell you herself, and Carter's going to rehab, so maybe now she can occupy her mind with something other than him." She pauses. "Why didn't you tell me the truth Livvie?"

"You didn't ask." I suddenly want to cry, "and Blythe wouldn't listen, nor Jackson. I wanted to tell you, but you already…"

"…Decided," She finishes for me. She closes her eyes. "I'm sorry… I just… You're a teenager and I had no idea what to expect. When I was your age, I did a couple of crazy things…" She stops. "I'm sorry Livvie, I really am."

When I don't say anything, she pulls me to her, giving me one of her sweet, perfumed hugs. "I'm sorry okay? Am I forgiven?"

"Yes." I whisper.

"I'm glad." She holds me for a few more moments before releasing me. "I wonder when Jackson will be here with his friend." She muses. "It's a girl, thank heavens. At least it means Jackson isn't still interested in that Lindsay."

"Or me." I almost say, suddenly sad as the relief from being exonerated is replaced by the overwhelming cocktail of feelings that wanting Jackson always brings out in me.

"I should go down and tell Mrs. Shannon that we're going to have a guest." She starts to get up.

"I'll do that." I offer, getting up from the couch, wanting nothing more than to escape any further mention of Jackson.

After I give Mrs. Shannon the message, I remain with her in the kitchen. She's the only one who never made me feel like an outcast, and in the past month, I've often found solace in her kitchen.

It's already evening when I hear the voices that tell me Jackson has arrived. I stiffen when I first hear his voice making introductions, and the sweet feminine voice of his companion as she laughs about something someone has said.

I'm slicing some fruit for Mrs. Shannon. Involuntarily, my fingers tighten around the knife.

"Don't cut off a finger in my kitchen because you have a crush." Mrs. Shannon says with a chuckle, "You never know, you may need it for when you really fall in love."

"I've fallen in love." The words are inside my head, but they're true, I've always belonged to Jackson, and regardless of whatever has happened, or what he thinks happened, he does belong to me. I may as well have spoken my thoughts aloud, as Mrs. Shannon shrugs and shakes her head. She goes back to her cooking, and I try to ignore the knowledge that Jackson is so close, and yet so far from me.

Maybe Blythe has told him what really happened, I think hopefully, or maybe Aunt Constance will. As for me, I can't risk facing the blatant disdain I saw in his eyes the last time I saw him, the regret in his expression because his desire for me was stronger than what he thought of me.

"Why don't you go out there and say hello, instead of hiding in here." Mrs. Shannon says at some point.

"I'm not hiding." I deny.

She snorts. "I know hiding when I see it."

I'm watching her finish dessert when I feel the tingle in my spine that can only mean one thing. I know Jackson is in the room. I keep my eyes on Mrs. Shannon, determined not to look at him, knowing I won't be able to bear the censure I'll see in his eyes.

"Mrs. S."

I hear his voice, and immediately my chest tightens.

Mrs. Shannon looks up over my head. "Jackson!" She smiles widely, responding to him the way everyone else does. "How's the big apple?"

"Big and crazy." He laughs, the rich sound floating

over me like a soft blanket.

Still I don't turn to look at him, but I can feel his eyes on me, as they exchange a few words of greeting over my head. I start to wonder, no to hope, that he would say something to me. I wait, but he doesn't even acknowledge me, after a few moments I hear him walk away.

"Now that was interesting." Mrs. Shannon says, when he's gone, leaving me reeling with the sorrow of his snub. "I feel as if I'm reading a new adult novel." she gives me a look that's full of compassion. "Why don't you go upstairs and get ready for dinner." She says. "You don't look too good."

"I'm fine." I emphasize the fine, but she gives me one of her arch looks. "I just have a headache." I sigh and get up from the kitchen stool I'm sitting on. "I'll just go lay down." I tell her. "In case anybody asks."

"Do you want a sandwich?"

I lost my appetite the moment Jackson decided to ignore me as if I wasn't even there. "No, I'm not hungry."

I stay in my room all through dinnertime. I can't hear what's going on downstairs, but I wonder if they'll miss me at the meal. Probably not, but I don't even care, nothing matters, not when Jackson hates me.

I lay on my back in my room with the lights off, staring at the ceiling in the dark. I find myself wondering about what will happen when I leave the house to go to college in the fall. Will Jackson totally forget about me? Will we become strangers? It makes me so sad. I hug my pillow and curl upon my side, closing my eyes tightly and trying my best not to cry. I'm still like that when the door opens, and the light comes on.

My heart soars when I see that it's Jackson, but it comes back down with a jarring thump almost immediately. His face is impersonal and expressionless, almost bored.

"Aunt Constance wanted to check on you," He says, without any inflection in his voice. He could be a stranger, not the Jackson I fell in love with. I wish I could be as uncaring as he obviously is. I wish I could suddenly not give a damn what he thinks of me. I wish the sight of him leaning on the door frame, looking so effortlessly perfect, and sexy didn't make me want to beg him to forgive me, even though I know I haven't done anything wrong.

I turn my gaze away from his perfection. "I'm fine." I mumble.

"So why didn't you come down for dinner."

I can feel his eyes on my face, but I don't look at him. "I wasn't hungry." I reply sullenly.

He enters the room and shuts the door behind him. "Really?"

"Yes."

"And you didn't bother to come meet Jessica." He states, "That was rude, don't you think?"

I don't care. I hate her already. I sit up on the bed and look at him. "Why did you bring her here?" I ask. Was it his way of telling me that it was over between us, and that he had moved on? "Is she your girlfriend now?"

He pauses for a long moment, his eyes on mine. "Maybe."

I inhale sharply. "Then I don't want to meet her."

"I suppose if it were Carter, or some other cute boy you could fool around with, you'd have been downstairs in a flash, wouldn't you?" His voice is cruel, "Tell me, was it just Carter you wanted or would any of the guys have done for your hungry little body? Cause it would be unfair for me to keep hating him if it could have been any one."

I feel tears stinging my eyes, and I blink fiercely, trying to keep the moisture inside. For so long, I'd dreamed of the kind of love Jackson and I would have, something total and absolute that would survive anything, but I'd been dreaming, basing my future on the nonsense in the romance novels. Hopelessness set in, and I feel the tears start to fall, staining my cheeks.

I hear Jackson sigh. "Olivia."

"Leave me alone," I cry, angry at myself for letting him see me cry. I toss the pillow I'm holding away and get up from the bed, facing him angrily, even though my cheeks are wet with tears. "Just go back to your Jennifer or Jessica or whatever her name is, I don't care."

At first he doesn't move, and then, so swiftly that I have no time to expect it, he's walking up to me and pulling me into his arms, kissing me through my tears. I want to stay angry, but instead, I surrender myself to the heat of his mouth on mine.

"You make me so fucking crazy." He mutters between kisses. He threads his finger through my hair, holding my head back, so I'm looking up at him. "What have you done to me?" His lips cover mine again and the next moment we're tearing at each other's clothes, hungrily devouring each other. I can't wait to feel him inside me, and it seems he can't either. He lays me back on the bed and kneels between my legs, pushing my skirt up around my waist while I undo his belt and zipper. I can hardly wait while he pulls out the small foil package from his wallet, puts it on, shoves my panties aside, and pushes into me with one firm thrust.

It's hot and fast and so good that I have to bite on my lip to keep from screaming loud enough for the whole house to come running. He groans as he slams into me again and again, his eyes closed and his head thrown back. In no time, uncontrollable pleasure suffuses my body, and I cry out helplessly, coming apart in his arms.

"I think I've gone insane," He says later, when we're still trying to catch our breaths. "You're like a siren, making me crazy." He pulls away from me and sits on the edge of the bed. "Is that what you want, helpless guys, so crazy about you they can't even think straight?"

"Jackson..." I start, "about Carter..."

"Just... stop." He says, a short, humorless laugh escaping his lips. "I don't want to know what you were playing at."

"But I love you," I blurt out, my hands at my neck fiddling with the platinum heart pendant he gave me. "I love you Jackson, so much."

He shakes his head and gets off the bed, "Not as much as I hate myself," he says cruelly.

I freeze, the rejection stunning and hurting me so badly, I can't even speak. I huddle in the bed while he puts on his clothes and leaves, turning off the light and closing the door behind him. I start to cry again, wondering if he really hates himself so much for being with me, or if he just said it to hurt me, and knowing that it makes no difference.

Book Two

Chapter Twelve

WE still haven't gone in for dinner. Elaine is describing some interesting fact she's discovered in her research on Halcyon, her smoky voice holding everyone's attention but mine. I can't stop thinking about the fact that Jackson is with Lindsay. They could very well be reigniting their adolescent relationship at the moment. I wonder how much, if anything, he knows of what she did. Did Blythe and Constance ever tell him that she had been behind everything that happened that night?

Would it even have mattered if they had? Over the years, I'd come to realize that the events of that night had probably been an excuse for him to end the clandestine relationship he was having with his family's charity case. It had been a way out for him, a way to leave me hanging without feeling the regret any decent man would have felt at crushing the illusions of the foolish girl I had been then.

He crushed more than my illusions. Would he be so hateful if he knew what his rejection had really cost me? I wonder sadly, my eyes going to the curtains at the French windows that open into the garden. I watch them move, slowly, almost dreamily, in the gentle breeze coming from outside. Well he would never know.

"What happened to Carter Felton?" I find myself asking Constance.

Constance sighs. "Blythe broke up with him after he told her the truth. I heard that he went to rehab in some place in California, and he decided to stay, he's a coach there now, helps people get over their addictions."

I nod. Apparently, it all worked out for everyone. Blythe must have gotten over him too. She had transferred to some university in France soon after I left Halcyon. When she came back a couple of years later, she had been quite popular in the New York society scene. Now she ran her own interior decorating firm and seemed to be doing very well. Everyone's wounds and bruises had healed, I decide. *Except for mine.*

No, mine are healed too, I remind myself. This house

I once loved, the people who own it, they mean nothing to me now. I'm not a lonely girl yearning for acceptance anymore. I'm an independent young woman with a career, and a full life. I keep this thought in my head as we all move to the dining room where Mrs. Shannon has laid out a sumptuous dinner. I allow myself to get lost in the taste of good food and wine. Who cares what Jackson and Lindsay Gorman are doing right now? I tell myself. I sure as hell don't.

After dinner, there's a lively discussion about the paintings in the house, from the various master's paintings in the main living room to the more contemporary ones hanging in the foyer. Carl surprises us all by having a seemingly inexhaustible supply of information about painters and paintings, from dates and places of birth and deaths to the occasionally incredible stories behind some of the art.

"I don't know why he sticks with you." I whisper to Nick, "He should be working in one of those swanky art galleries or auction houses."

"He used to." Nick says. "It went bankrupt, I think. Anyway he meets a lot more people working for me," He grins, "and yes, by people, I mean women."

I shake my head, and listen as Elaine tries to match her

knowledge of art against Carl's. After a while, I get up and go out through the French doors, onto the terrace overlooking the garden. There's a carved stone railing between the terrace and the garden, and I lean on it, enjoying the summer sounds of the night around me.

"So you and Jackson Lockewood…" I don't hear Nick until he's right beside me. "What's the story?"

I don't look at him. "What makes you think there's one?"

"Come on." He chuckles and leans down on the railing beside me. "Anyone could see the sparks flying from miles away. Were you in love with him?"

I snort. It's a harsh, bitter sound. "As much in love as a teenage girl could be."

"And he took advantage of you… what a bastard."

"No, I… It wasn't like that." Even after everything, I don't want anyone to think that Jackson took advantage of me, because he didn't. I'd wanted him, and I would have given him every part of me without him having to ask. "He never did anything I didn't want desperately."

I can feel Nick's eyes on me, and when I turn to face him, there's compassion in his gaze, and understanding. "Love is so short," he quotes solemnly, "forgetting takes forever."

Exactly, I think. How I've wished at times that I could flip a switch and forget that I ever loved Jackson, but I know I'll never forget him. "What do you think of the house?" I ask, changing the subject.

His eyes gleam. "It's a treasure." He says. I've been talking with Elaine. There's so much material here, the history of the house, the land, the architect, the influences, the changes and additions over the years, the exquisite art collection and furniture, and the people who have lived here. It's going to read almost like fiction, but with images. Gilt wants the book to be interesting, not just a collection of photographs of famous houses.

"Well that certainly explains Elaine." I say, "Grace told me that she's been quite successful writing short stories."

"She might look like a model but she's as sharp as a needle, too sharp to fall for an old lothario like me, anyway."

"Good for her," I say teasingly, "she deserves better than you, every girl does."

"Don't go around telling them that." He laughs, and then surprisingly pulls me towards him for a quick hug. "You'll be all right here, won't you? Jackson being here won't be too much of an issue?"

"I'm big girl, Nick."

"Good." He smiles.

I enjoy his good humor because I know it'll only be for a short while. Tomorrow he'll be a tyrant, yelling at Carl, and giving me cryptic instructions on the exact messages he wants the images to convey, expecting me to be able to read his mind and see the picture exactly as he does, and get my camera to give it to him exactly as he saw it in his mind. However, I don't mind, I'm even excited. If there is anything that has brought me comfort in the last few years, it's been my work.

The sound of a car on the drive disturbs the silence outside. "Well, that's probably the big bad Jackson." Nick observes. He looks at me. "Don't hide out here because of him. You only defeat your demons by facing them."

Only, some demons cannot be defeated, I think sadly. "I'm not hiding, Nick. I'm enjoying the night air."

He laughs and goes back inside. The breeze picks up, bringing with it the scent of the flowers in the garden. I inhale, remembering the peonies and tulips Constance used to grow and wondering if she still gave the gardeners trouble with her strict instruction on exactly how to plant them.

I thought I had forgotten this place. The realization that I never really did causes a small ache in my chest. For a moment, I allow myself to mourn the life Jackson and I could have had. The love I thought we had when I used to dream of living here with him, of watching my children grow up in the house I loved.

How foolish I was! I think, snapping out of the thoughts. How idiotic to have thought that there would be any happy ever after for Jackson Lockewood and pathetic orphan who depended on his family for a home.

I don't want to go back into the living room, so I

descend the steps from the terrace into the garden and follow the stone path past the meticulously maintained patterns of flowers and shrubs. I keep to the lit up path, walking aimlessly for a while, knowing but not wanting to acknowledge where ultimately, my legs are leading me.

I round the corner of the house, and there it is, just the way I remember, the lily pond, now covered with the wide green leaves, and the gazebo in the distance, small, quiet, and lit only by the lights around the house. I pause, unsure whether to proceed, whether I dare disturb and revisit the memories that were made inside that small place.

My legs carry me forward, and I walk up the stone steps into the small space. It looks exactly the same, empty except for the seats along the walls, and clean, except for a few stray leaves that must have been blown in by the wind.

I almost turn back. What did I hope to achieve by coming here? Already my head is being assaulted by the memories I've followed here, memories like a 'voiceless ghost,' leading me up cliffs, and down, till I'm lonely and lost.

Chuckling ruefully at the sad poetry that's snuck into my head, I make my way to one of the seats and settle into it. Over the dwarf wall, I can see the pond, and I watch the wide, dark leaves float over the surface, and here and there, the pink bursts of color where a lily is blooming.

I sit there lost in my thoughts for a while, until the sound of footsteps breaks me out of my reverie. I look up to see Jackson walking towards me with that firm, long, stride. He's wearing a dress shirt, unbuttoned at the collar, and black trousers that accentuate his long legs and lean figure. His hair is slightly disheveled, just enough to make him look even sexier than he usually does. The moonlight and the lights from the house cast shadows across his features that move as he walks, emphasizing the angles of his face and giving him a hard and implacable expression.

I don't want to admire him, so I look away, back to the flowers on the pond. Why is he here?

He stops at the entrance and leans on the frame, watching me silently for what seems like an eternity. Still I refuse to look at him. If he followed me here, then he must have a reason, something to say perhaps. Well, I'm not going to be the one to draw it out of him.

"I see what you're doing," He says softly, so soft that I almost don't hear the words. "You are leading me on; to the spots we knew when we haunted here together." He pauses, and smiles, obviously pleased with himself for remembering the line from one of my favorite poems, the same one coincidentally, that I had been thinking of a moment ago. Is he really a demon then, one who can read my mind?

"Well," He continues when I don't reply, "How does

it feel to revisit olden haunts at last?"

I shrug, unwilling to give him the satisfaction of acknowledging that any memories of importance reside here for me. "How did your dinner go?" I ask conversationally.

He replies with a small dismissive movement of his shoulders. "There was food, and there was Lindsay. It seems her parents suddenly had to visit a friend in town."

"How convenient." The words escape me before I can put on my verbal filter.

He chuckles. "You're very imaginative." He says, looking slightly amused. "In your head, does she get her parents out of the way so she can me serve dinner on her naked body?"

The image, coupled with what I imagine his response would have been, fills me with a sudden, unreasonable surge of jealousy.

"Neither you nor Lindsay feature very much in my head." I retort sharply.

"Hmmm," The small sound manages to convey both disbelief and dismissal. "You must be very forgiving," he says, "if you've managed to forget that she convinced her brother to assault you." He's watching me as he speaks. "I was not so forgiving when I found out. Carter's beautiful face will always be ruined by a broken nose, and Lindsay," he grins almost malevolently, "I doubt she'll be inviting me over again anytime soon."

I swallow, disbelief making me confused. "How long have you known?" I ask.

"The day after you ran away." He folds his arms over his chest, but his eyes remain on my face. "Constance was worried that you'd left because she hadn't given you a chance to defend yourself. She told me everything."

"Then why…" I stop myself before I can complete the sentence, ashamed of what I'd been about to say. Why did you let me think you hated me all this time for something you know I never did? Why did you never come to find me? Why did you let me suffer all these years when you knew the truth?

But I don't ask, because the answer is obvious. He hadn't cared enough. My departure had probably been his way out from a relationship he knew was going nowhere.

"Why what?" he's looking at me as if he knows what I'm thinking.

I shake my head. "Nothing," I say. "She did us both a favor, didn't she? If not for her we'd have spent a lot more time on a relationship that ultimately meant nothing."

I can't read the expression on his face as he pushes off the frame and moves towards me, coming to sit facing me. To anyone looking at us from outside, we would seem like lovers having a private conversation in a romantic setting, but it couldn't be farther from the truth.

"I'm sure she'll be glad to hear that," he says, "although maybe she shouldn't have bothered. If it meant so little then it probably would have fizzled out very quickly on its own."

"Yes," I agree softly, knowing that I'm lying to him, and to myself. Seven years, and still, nothing has fizzled out for me. I'm still as affected by his presence as I ever was. His eyes are intense as they study my face, and I suspect that I've not fooled him with my lie. I find myself wishing he hadn't come to sit so close to me. I can feel the heat from his body, and the faint scent of his aftershave teasing my nostrils. And his eyes, they're like a spell, holding me captive, so I can't look away from the challenge and the invitation I see in them.

I want to hold his gaze, and return the challenge in his eyes with indifference in my own, but my heart is pounding, and my hands are suddenly trembling, even my mind is betraying me, supplying me with images from my memories. Images of those eyes filled with desire for me, memories of those lips on my skin, my neck, my lips…

Abruptly, I get up from the seat. "It's late." I say, "I should go inside."

Immediately, he's standing too, towering over me. We were sitting close, and now we're standing even closer. My eyes are level with the top of his chest, and I can feel the soft tickle of his breath on my forehead. Suddenly, I can't move anymore, my legs feel too weak.

He reaches out and places a finger under my chin, lifting my face up to look at him. I tremble even at the small touch, and I can see the gleam in his eyes that tells me he noticed.

"You shouldn't have come back, Olivia," he says, the softness of the words, doing nothing to temper the threat in them.

I don't argue, even I know that I shouldn't have come back, not when he can still make me feel like this.

"Well, hopefully I won't be here for long." That's the reply on my lips, but he doesn't let me say the words, as soon as I open my mouth, he leans forward and covers my lips with his.

I can't think. I can't feel anything apart from the

touch of his lips as they claim mine, and the hardness of his body against my own. My nose fills with his scent even as my skin responds to his touch. Soon it feels as if all my senses have been possessed by him.

I don't want this, I think desperately. I don't want this unbearable pleasure, the fluttering in my stomach, the warm pulsing heat in my core. I don't want to feel this insane desire to reach out and run my fingers over his chest, to lose myself in his kiss. I don't want to still be in love with him.

It takes all my self-control and willpower, but I brace my hands on his chest and push off from him, stepping as far away from him as I can.

"It must be really bad if your charms didn't work on Lindsay and you have to settle for me tonight." I say caustically. My chest is heaving, and my lips are tingling sweetly, desperate for more, but I'd rather die than let him know that.

He's also breathing deeply, but at my words, he laughs. "You know better than to doubt my charms, Olivia"

I do, but I'd rather not dwell on that. I close my eyes against the unwanted memories. "Goodnight Jackson." I say, walking away from him. "I'm going to bed."

He doesn't make any move to stop me, and as I

walk towards the house, I can feel his eyes on my back, and taste the sweetness of his kiss lingering on my lips.

Chapter Thirteen

AFTER a night spent tossing and turning, I'm up early the next morning. I take a shower and dress simply in dark pants and a cream top, securing my hair in a ponytail. Downstairs, I follow the familiar smell of brewing coffee to the breakfast room, a large, airy room close to the kitchens where until noon, there's always coffee, eggs, and toast.

Neither Constance nor Mrs. Shannon are anywhere to be found, but Nick is at the table, staring morosely into the steaming mug of coffee in front of him. Carl is wolfing down a plate of bacon and eggs, while Elaine is at the end of the table, typing into her tiny laptop. Jackson isn't anywhere in the room, so I release the breath I hadn't known I was holding, and join them.

"Good morning," I say to everyone and no one in particular.

"Good morning." Carl says with his mouth full. Elaine raises a hand in a halfhearted wave and Nick just grunts. What a cheerful bunch! I think, pouring myself some coffee from the pot and watching as Nick takes a sip of his. Before the mug is half-empty, he'll be fully awake and his tyranny will no doubt begin.

"What happened to you last night?" Elaine says suddenly, looking up from her typing. "You disappeared right after dinner."

"Yeah, I went for a walk in the garden, then upstairs to bed."

"Oh." She gives me a suspicious look. "Well I and Nick did some planning for the article. He has a list of the pictures he wants."

I look towards Nick. His mug is still almost full. "Nick? Do you want to let me know what you want so I can start working on it?"

"Yes," He groans, "just let me wake up first."

I hide a smile behind my mug. "I thought Jackson was going to show you guys the original plans of the house today." I ask Elaine.

"Oh, that." Her hair swings as she shakes her head.

"We had to take a rain check. He's left, gone back to the city."

"Oh." The small exclamation escapes me. He had gone back to the city. I feel a mixture of relief and disappointment. I had prepared myself for days of him being around, and now he was just gone. What an anticlimax. And proof that my presence here means nothing to him.

Well, his absence means nothing to me, I decide resolutely. He is nothing to me really, just some guy I loved a long time ago. Relationships end and people who love each other sometimes grow out of it, as we would have grown out of our feelings too, in time. Then this sense of an unresolved affair wouldn't be part of my life.

Still I can't help asking myself why he came at all. Was it just to see what the years without him had done to me, or to test me, and see if he could still take advantage of my attraction to him. Well, I had survived the years without him, and hopefully, I'd convinced him that physically, he was nothing to me. So there was nothing left for him at Halcyon if I had been the reason he came in the first place.

"Constance will be showing us the plans and the sculptures in the garden." Elaine continues, just then she looks towards the door. "Oh, here she is. Good morning Constance."

"Good morning." Constance walks into the room and

stops at the table. "I hope you have everything you need."

"Yes, thank you." Nick puts aside his morning bad humor to reply.

She turns to me. "Jackson's left." Her eyes are searching my face, almost as if she thinks I had something to do with his leaving.

"I heard." I reply, giving nothing away.

She sighs. "Oh well. Enjoy your work."

As I predicted, as soon as Nick has taken a significant amount of coffee, he's wide awake and itching to get as much work done as fast as possible. Immediately after breakfast, we start working. Nick is in his element, aside from developing a storyboard that follows the history of the house from its design to the inhabitants through the years, and to the present day; he has also drawn up a list of all the scenes that will go with the story.

We discuss the article and exchange ideas, while I schedule the pictures over the next few days according to the time of day I think would fit the scenery best. I spend the rest of the day taking most of the external pictures, taking advantage of the good weather.

Every morning, I meet with Nick and Elaine after breakfast, and afterwards, when they go to talk to Constance or look through old family history, I start to work, usually right through lunch, and sometimes almost to dinnertime. Taking pictures for me has always been a solitary affair, and it keeps my mind occupied. Keeping my mind on my work helps to keep it off Jackson, and the less I think of him, the better.

Thankfully, nobody else brings him up for conversation. So while I work, I can almost pretend as if that first day didn't really happen. I can wake up, take my pictures, go to bed, and look forward to returning to my normal life without having to acknowledge how affected I was by seeing Jackson again.

"You know, sometimes in situations like this, you end up asking yourself what you ever saw in him." May's voice is contemplative on the phone. "You spend years thinking you never got over them, and then one meeting and you realize the feelings are all gone.

I think of the feeling of Jackson's lips on mine, the way his hands had burned my skin where he touched me. I'd wanted more than that kiss. I'd wanted to rekindle all the memories of what I knew he could do to my body. But that was only physical, I tell myself. It didn't mean I still had any feelings for him.

"You're right," I reply. I've just taken a shower after a hard day spent photographing the gardens, first in the early morning light, and then in the afternoon, and much later in the early evening light. I'd returned to my room exhausted and grimy. I almost fell asleep in the shower, and right now May's voice on the phone is the only thing keeping me awake. I'm even contemplating skipping dinner and just sleeping until morning.

"So do you think you've gotten over him?"

I sigh. "I don't know. Seeing him again, it made me start to think of what I used to dream our lives would be like."

"Do you still find him attractive?"

I laugh bitterly. "Physically? Of course. I'd have to be blind and deaf not to find him attractive."

I hear her chuckle. "Yeah, he was always hot as hell."

"Still is."

"Maybe you should sleep with him," She suggests. "Fuck him all night and get it out of your system."

"I'm sure it will take more than one night to get Jackson out of my system."

"Well then, as many nights as it takes, at least you'll be having fun."

And after that? What if I can't get him out of my system? What then? Another few years of longing, of wanting something I can't have? "Too late May, He's gone back to the New York."

"Then when he returns, make him give you a few orgasms, for my sake." She laughs. "Seriously, you wouldn't believe how horny being pregnant makes me. Chace is beginning to avoid me. That's how insatiable I've become."

"Eeeew!" I laugh. "TMI, May, I don't want to know."

I'm still laughing when I hear the soft knock on the door. My first thought is that it's Jackson, and after a few moments of panic, and wondering how quickly I can change out of my thigh length t-shirt into something decent, I realize that Jackson would never knock. He would just walk in as if he owned the place, and whoever was in it, in this case, me.

"Who is it?" I call out.

The door opens a crack, and a familiar blonde head appears.

"Livvie?" Her voice is hesitant.

"Blythe?" I frown. I had known that she might come, but seeing her so suddenly, for the first time in so many years, it still surprises me.

The door opens fully and she enters the room. She looks almost the same, except that now some of her care-free air has been replaced with a Constance-like softness and serenity. Her hair is in a clip at her nape, and her pale blue dress is simple, but stylish and tasteful.

She smiles. "I hope you don't mind, but I couldn't wait for you to come downstairs."

"I... no of course not." I'm still standing in the middle of my room. I should be more welcoming, but I can't help feeling hesitant, after all, I haven't seen her in years. It feels odd that someone I used to be so close to is now practically a stranger.

"I can't believe how long it's been." She says. "How are you? You look wonderful." She's still smiling, but I can sense that she's waiting for me to put her at ease, to show that I still don't resent her for what happened seven years ago.

"You look great too." I smile back and move towards her so we can exchange a quick hug.

"When Aunt Constance told me you were going to be here photographing the house, I thought it was so apt, considering how much you always loved it. She said she would be here to make sure everything was in order, and I thought that perhaps I should drop by while you're here. How's it been?"

I shrug and go to sit on the bed. "Okay. I've mostly been working."

"Yes." She pauses. "Jackson was here."

I nod, wondering why she's bringing him up, but her face gives nothing away. "Mrs. Shannon said he hardly ever comes here anymore."

"No, he doesn't." She moves to the window, staring down at the front of the house. "I've missed this place. " She sighs. "Sometimes I forget what it's like, and I start to think I'm in love with life in the city, and then I come back, and it's like I'm really home."

I think I know what she means. Halcyon is the home of her childhood and her memories.

"Jackson wasn't interested in the article until Aunt Constance mentioned that you would be here to do the pictures." She turns back to face me. "He came here to see you."

I put on my best expression of incredulity. "Why would he do that?"

Blythe rolls her eyes in a gesture that's so out of keeping with her elegant appearance that I almost laugh. "You don't have to pretend with me Livvie." She sighs. "At first I was so angry at you, I didn't stop to think. And even when Carter told me the truth, I was too angry with him, to wonder why Lindsay did it. But when I started to think about it, it was clear that was never about me, or Carter, It was always about you and Jackson."

When I don't say anything, she continues. "I tried to ask him, but he wouldn't even talk about you." She shakes her head. "Like the sound of your name was an insult. When in the months that followed, he wouldn't even come here at all, I knew for sure, even if I didn't have any proof." She pauses "I was right, wasn't I? There was something going on between you and Jackson."

I shrug. "It was a long time ago Blythe."

"Not long enough," She says, coming to sit beside me on the bed, "If you're the only thing that could make him come back here."

"Not for long though." I reply drily, "He was only here for a day.

She chuckles. "He'll be back before you leave, I'm sure."

"I hope not." I look at her squarely. "I don't know what you're thinking, but I don't want to relive any aspect of the past. I just want to do my job and go home."

"Oh." She looks disappointed. "Oh okay. I just... I hoped ..."

"That there was some romantic happy ending on the way?"

"Well, you deserve it, after everything."

"Life doesn't work that way."

She sighs. "I'm so sorry Livvie, for everything."

It's not the first time she's apologizing. When I left Halcyon the first time and moved to Chace's new apartment in the city, she'd come to see me, sorry for the way she'd reacted, the things she's said, and hopeful that I wouldn't hold it against her. I told her not to worry, but forgiving her, and becoming best friends again as if nothing had happened were two different things, especially when every day I had to deal with the pain that only I knew I was bearing, the pain of losing the man I thought was the love of my life.

"It's okay," I reply. "Really."

"There's so much I didn't know then, and I was so in love with Carter, I never stopped to ask you if what he said was true."

"Blythe, it doesn't matter."

"No, it does." She swallows. "I was arrogant, and the idea that you would be even a little jealous of me, enough to try to take something of mine, was easy to believe. I'd convinced myself that I thought of you as an equal, but deep down I still felt superior because I was *Blythe Lockewood.*" She shakes her head.

I smile. "Don't over think it, Blythe. It was ages ago."

She draws in a long breath. "Well, let me leave you to get ready for dinner."

"Yeah," I pause. "What about Carter? Constance told me that you…"

"Broke up with him? I did. I loved him Livvie, but I just had to accept that I deserved better than the guy he was that night."

I don't say anything, so she continues. "He's a coach at the rehab place he went seven years ago. He'll probably never leave." She sighs. "I'm glad he found his place, as I found mine, running my business and all that."

So we all found our place, I think soberly. Only sometimes, I still feel like I'm floating around, looking for a place to anchor, and knowing that there's only one place for me, and only one person I want to be with.

I can't keep thinking like that if I want to convince myself that I've gotten over Jackson, so I shake the thought from my head. "I'll meet you downstairs." I tell Blythe.

She nods. "It was nice to see you Livvie."

"You too, Blythe."

.

Chapter Fourteen

ALTHOUGH I like to work in the privacy of my room, sometimes, after walking around the house and grounds taking pictures, I go to the library to work on developing some of the digital shots. The floor to ceiling bookshelves are stacked with thousands of books, many of which I spent my teenage years reading.

I love working with cameras, bur I relish the part where I embellish beautiful images with magical software, to add the little things that take a scene from beautiful to incredible. I'm so engrossed in what I'm doing that I don't hear the door to the library opening.

"Hey you," Nick's voice interrupts my work. He's standing by the door, looking every inch the modern metro-sexual male in gray pants and a cream shirt.

"Hey you too," I turn back to my work. We're almost done, and in two days, we'll all leave Halcyon. I can't wait to leave, not because I've not enjoyed being around Constance or Blythe, or Mrs. Shannon, which I have, but because, the sooner I'm done and gone, the sooner I'll stop worrying about Jackson coming back to disturb my feelings again.

"Elaine's come up with a fantastic first draft," He says. "Reads like a good novel, which is what Grace wanted." He sighs. "God knows another academic sounding book on architectural styles would have bored me to death."

"I'm looking forward to reading it."

He shrugs. "You should. By the way, did you know the Lockewoods gave an engagement party for a minor European royal in the twenties and the next day the fiancée eloped with the younger son?"

"Guy Lockewood." I smile. "He was a pilot, riding on the glories from being a flyboy in the war. Fortunately, it didn't cause another battle of Troy. She came to her senses and went back to her fiancé."

Nick looks at me intently. "I forget you know all about the family history. You did grow up here after all. I still can't believe you never mentioned that. It rankles."

"You'll get over it." I laugh. "Seriously, it's just not

something I talk about that much."

"I get that," he laughs. "Though I'll be more likely to forgive you if you promise to tell Blythe all the wonderful things you know about me."

"I don't know any wonderful things about you."

He gives me a poisonous look, but I only smile wider. "I'm not going to be your wingman here, if that's what you're thinking. I thought it was Elaine you were interested in."

"I'm interested in all women." He shakes his head, "In any case Elaine's more interested in the owner of this lovely house than she is in a poor old journalist like me. I don't think a day has gone by when she doesn't ask Constance when the guy is coming back."

"And is he planning to, come back, I mean."

"I have no idea," He says distantly, his mind already on something else. "I should leave you to work." He leaves the room, shutting the door behind him.

I don't care what happens between Jackson and Elaine, I tell myself, as long as it happens when I'm safely away from Halcyon, as long as he doesn't come back to disturb my peace of mind again. Offering a silent prayer to whatever is keeping him away, I turn my attention back to the picture on my computer.

I'm still working when the door opens again. "I thought you were going to leave me to finish my work." I say playfully, mimicking Nick's accent without looking up.

He doesn't reply. In the silence that follows, my fingers pause on the mouse, and I feel the familiar tingle going down my spine. Immediately, I know it's not Nick, but Jackson, that I've somehow conjured him out of my thoughts, and he's back to torment me again.

Still I don't look up, I don't want to see him and acknowledge that he has returned, not when I hope he would disappear, not when despite the fact that I thought I didn't want him to come back, my heart is pounding with excitement.

"Are you going to ignore me until I go away?" His voice is smooth, teasing even. I listen to his footsteps as he walks closer, until he's standing right in front of me.

I look up at him, my expression deliberately insolent, resisting with all my strength, the urge to gawk at how delicious he looks. He's wearing a suit, and dark one, with a pinstriped blue shirt underneath. The tie is missing, and the first button at the collar is open, exposing the column of his throat. It's amazing how much I want to reach for him, how much I want to get up and wrap my arms around his waist, press my lips to the warm skin at his neck. For a moment, I'm filled with a strong urge to forget that we're separated by this ocean of hurt and memories, to imagine instead that we're still in love, and he's come home to me, the woman he loves, who would waste no time in showing him how much she's missed him.

However, that's not how we are, and that ocean of hurt and memories will never go away. I take a deep breath.

"I didn't know you were coming back." I say, dragging my eyes away from him.

"You hoped I wasn't."

Could he read my mind? "I just assumed you'd rather be far away than be forced to endure my company." I accompany the words with a saccharine smile.

He looks amused, and I watch uneasily as he comes closer and drops to an elegant squat in front of me "You're not wrong." He states mildly.

He is too close. I swallow, nervous and excited at the same time. "Then why are you here?"

His gray eyes are burning into mine. I feel like I'm being held prisoner, part of me would like nothing more than to escape, but the other part would trade a lot to have him so close for all time. I wait for him to say something in reply to my question.

"Because," he says softly, his fingers reaching for my hair to move a few locks behind my ear, "There's also a part of me that wants to be around you."

I shiver from his touch and move my head until his fingers are no longer touching me, "Aren't you a glutton for punishment?" My voice is shaking.

His brow rises questioningly, and I almost sigh. *Why on earth does he have to be so beautiful?* "If I am, then what about you?" he asks, "Nobody forced you to come back here."

"I already told I didn't know you'd be here, Jackson."

"For a long time I couldn't bear to be." There is a small smile on his lips as he looks at me. "You ruined this house for me, Olivia. Did you know that? You turned it from a home into a store of painful memories."

Had the events of seven years ago really affected him that much? It's hard to think so, considering how easily he had abandoned me. After I left Halcyon, for a long time, I hoped that one day he would show up and tell me that he loved me, that he couldn't live without me, I hoped for an opportunity to vindicate myself, to heal the love that I thought we had.

But he never came. I went through the worst period of my life alone, and he went on to be a rising star in the business and investment world, eventually conquering it, and multiplying his family fortunes while dating high profile women who appeared with him in society columns.

If he had cared enough about me to abandon Halcyon because of memories of us, then why had he never tried to find me?

"One more reason for you to hate me then," I say flippantly, dismissing my train of thought. There was no use obsessing about the past. "My offences are many aren't they, if seven years haven't been long enough to dull them in your memories."

He laughs, surprising me. "You're so nonchalant about the past." He says mildly, "Does it really mean so little to you? Or are you just pretending?" His eyes move down to my lips, then back up to hold my eyes again. "That's why I came back here at all, the thought of you coming to Halcyon as if you don't care, as if the past means nothing. I had to come and see for myself."

"And now you've seen." I say, trying not be affected by his nearness. I remove the laptop from my lap and set it on the coffee table by the chair, just to have something to do to keep my hands busy while he's so close. "The past are just that, past, it means nothing to me, and it shouldn't mean anything to you either."

He rises to his feet, taking hold of my arms and pulling me up with him. Now we're standing toe to toe, and it's definitely much too close for me.

"I know you're lying." He says softly.

"No, you want to think I'm lying because it's so impossible for anyone to get over the unsurpassable Jackson Lockewood. Well guess what, I'm not Lindsay Gorman, and I don't want anything to do with you."

My outburst seems to amuse him. "Really?"

"Yes," I sigh, "I don't care anymore about what happened in the past. I've moved on."

"That's the thing," He says. *Why is his voice so soft?* "I don't believe you."

"Believe what you want."

We're still facing each other, eye to eye. I pour all the indifference I can muster into my expression, and hope that he will back down. He doesn't. Instead, he keeps looking at me with that small taunting playing on his lips.

"I will." His hand moves along my arm, his fingers drawing a teasing line down to my wrist, and against all my control, my body trembles.

His lips quirk in a smile of triumph. "See, Olivia, that's me proving that you're lying."

"That's you proving nothing."

"Okay," He pauses. "So if against all my better judgment, I decide to kiss you now, you won't feel anything." His eyes dig into mine, "right?"

"What I feel, is that you shouldn't go against your better judgment."

"Someone should have said that to me eight years ago, before I ever laid a finger on you. Think of all we could have avoided."

"Yes." I say. Why do I feel so unreasonably hurt that he would wish that what is still the happiest time of my life never happened?

"My better judgment didn't stop me then, and it won't stop me now either, Olivia. I want to kiss you and watch you feel nothing in my arms. Maybe then I won't be consumed by the thought of what it would be like after all these years." His eyes drop to my lips, "What do you think?"

I'm not thinking anymore. My lips are tingling with anticipation. I run my tongue over them, only realizing afterwards, when I see his eyes follow the movement hungrily, that I shouldn't have. "I think you shouldn't." I whisper. Why am I so conflicted? I should storm out of the room. He could block my way, but I doubt he would hold me against my will. So what am I still doing here, standing in front on him, watching him while he drives me to uncontrollable lust?

A finger moves underneath my chin, lifting my face

up to his. "You're not afraid, are you?"

I shake my head. "What is there to be afraid of?"

He laughs softly, "Yes, what?" he says, moments before his lips descend on mine.

.

Chapter Fifteen

I resist the urge to moan and relax against him. That's what he wants, for me to let down my guard and give away the fact that I still want him, but I'd rather die than give him the satisfaction. I'd rather let the fire raging inside me, the need growing like hot flames in my core, to burn me to ashes rather than give in to it. I'm no longer the seventeen year old girl who didn't know any better than to say yes to her body's desires. I can say no.

Nothing good can come from rekindling what we had in the past, I think, desperately holding on to my control as Jackson's lips draw a sensuous path over mine. Already my nipples are stiff, my core clenching with need, and I can feel moisture gathering between my legs. I could just give in, the traitorous voice in my head says, enjoy the pleasure, once, twice, as many times as I can in the two days before I have to leave, or even after, as many times as it takes to get this insane desire for him out of my system.

Only I know that no matter how many times, it would never be enough. It won't assuage the hunger that has been building for years, the hunger that has now exploded in my body. Instinct tells me that Jackson will not be satisfied with just my physical surrender to him. He won't be satisfied until he had fulfilled his desire to prove to himself that he left a mark on me that can't be erased. If only he knew

My thoughts keep me from falling victim to the slow, seduction of his kiss, the helpless desire I feel as his tongue licks over my lips, slipping inside my mouth to caress my own, the heat from his hands as they moves slowly up and down my arm, around my waist, and up to my breasts. I let him kiss me while I hold myself still, swallowing every moan growing in my throat and battling every ache of desire that urges me to respond.

Even the memories I've tortured myself with all these years do not do him any justice, I think through my fog of arousal, as his fingers find a pebbled nipple through my clothes. I have to bite back a sigh when he brushes his finger back and forth over it, causing a persistent, sweet ache between my thighs, a pulsing need for nothing more than to take this pleasure to the end.

He releases my lips, and his eyes are triumphant as he looks at me. "You may pretend all you want, but your body can't lie. I know the meaning of the flush staining your skin, Olivia. I know why your heart is racing." His fingers brush over my nipple again, then he pinches it lightly, just enough to send a sweet pulse of pleasure to my brain, and this time, a moan escapes me.

"You're not as uninterested as you pretend," He continues, "Whatever you've convinced yourself in your head, your body hasn't forgotten."

"It's only sex," I say, lifting my chin, trying my best to keep up an appearance of dignity, pride even. I try to sound as dismissive as I can, "and I've discovered since I left here that there are any number of men with hands and mouths that can make my skin flush and my heart race.

The tightening of his jaw is almost imperceptible. "Are you trying to make me jealous?"

"No, I'm trying to make you leave me alone."

"Hmmm." He draws out the sound, and when I'm not expecting it, he lowers his head and kisses me again, this time, a soft kiss at the corner of my mouth. "It's not working." He says, his warm breath warming the skin of my face. "I still want to do this." He kisses me again, using his tongue to caress my bottom lip before delving inside to taste my own. "And this," He releases my lips to trail kisses across my cheeks, my eyelids, making me so weak I can barely stand. "I still want to take off your clothes and bury myself in your sweet, responsive body. I still want to indulge myself in you, until I'm no longer haunted by the scent of your skin in my nose everywhere I go, the memory of the feel of your body, your breasts that fit so perfectly in my hands." He pauses to place one last kiss on my lips, "after seven years of carrying all that around, I deserve some relief, don't I? I deserve a chance to find out if the reality lives up to the memories."

"Well you're not going to." I manage shakily. The images he has conjured in my head are so graphic, I can hardly keep myself from tearing off his clothes. I need to get away, I think. I need a cold shower, because at this point, I'm one step away from stripping and spreading my legs right here in the library so he can give me the relief my body is dying for

I push away from him and pick up my laptop, holding it like a shield between him and me. "I'm not interested in making myself available so you can prove to yourself that I still want you."

"I don't have to prove anything, sweetheart. I already know. You can run all you want. It doesn't change what your body wants."

I manage a shaky laugh. "I'm not running away, I'm

staying away from you, because I have better things to do than to argue about what my body does or doesn't want."

"Arguing is the least of things I want to do with you, Olivia." His smile is charming and persuasive, "Let me give you what you want."

What I want is for him to love me. That's all I've wanted since I first met him. That's all I've wanted even in the years I've spent without him, trying to get over him. I want him to listen when I tell him everything that's happened, to offer me the comfort I've wanted for years that only he can give me, to banish all the ghosts that still haunt me.

But he doesn't want to give me comfort. He wants to take, to subjugate my body until the anger he's carried around all these years is spent. Will I enjoy the subjugation? Probably. But then what? A new cycle of hurt and pain?

"You can't give me what I want." I tell him.

He takes a step towards me. "Try me."

Why does he look so earnest? The smile is gone, and looking at him, I can almost convince myself that he means something more than just sex. I swallow painfully.

"Olivia..."

I don't hear what he's about to say, because, at that moment, the door opens, and Elaine walks into the room.

"Oh, Jackson!" She exclaims, practically simpering. "I had no idea you were back."

When he turns to her, the intense expression leaves his face, replaced by the charm that is the face he shows to the world. "I only just arrived." He tells her.

She frowns. "Really, I was right outside, I didn't see you come in."

"That's because I brought my boat." His smile at her is almost indulgent, "and I came in through the back."

Her eyes widen as the sophisticated mask drops. "A boat! Wow! Do I get to see it?"

"Of course."

I tune out of their conversation after that. He walks towards her and they keep talking and laughing. I may as well not be in the room.

I leave them and go upstairs to my room. Outside, the day is turning to twilight, and the light from the setting sun is creating some beautiful effects with the few clouds in the darkening sky.

I should take a picture, I think, but I don't. I don't reach for my camera. Instead, I keep looking outside until the sun is nothing more than a faint grayness in the west.

Soon it will be dinnertime, and I'll have to go downstairs and make conversation regardless of the turmoil bubbling inside me. I'll sit at a table with Jackson and try to be civil even though I hate him so much and yet love him even more.

How could I have thought that I could come here without any consequences? That Jackson would let me do my work in peace without using his many advantages to revert me to the helpless girl who left here seven years ago.

How could I have thought I was over him? That's the biggest lie I've told myself through the years, because I'll never be over him. I'm always going to want him. To lose hold on all my senses whenever he's near because whether he knows it or not, he did leave a mark on me.

I wish I could leave, abandon my assignment and run away from Halcyon like I did seven years ago, but I won't give him that satisfaction. For two more days, I can look him in the eye and pretend, yes pretend that he means nothing to me.

Maybe it's the memory of the first time I left Halcyon, but I'm suddenly seized with a desire to see my old room. I go outside to the corridor and make my way towards the other wing, where the master suite and the other family room are located. The door to the room is unlocked. I push it open, expecting it to have changed in some way, to have been redecorated to match any one of the other unused room in the house.

But it's exactly the same. It's almost as if I only just stepped out, and my eighteen year old self will return at any moment, to her books, her posters, and her bed.

I close my eyes as the flood of memories engulfs me. All the scenes from all those years ago, and Jackson, always Jackson, making love to me, teasing me, and talking about his plans, for himself, for us. In here, the memories are alive.

I push them away and continue inside. It's surprisingly clean, with none of the dust one would expect from a space that hasn't been used in a long time. I go to sit on the bed, feeling the soft mattress gives way underneath me. Again all those bittersweet memories from a lifetime ago fill my mind.

Will I ever forget, I wonder. Will there ever come a time when I'll remember Jackson and feel nothing? When I'll find happiness in the arms of some other man who will make me forget that I ever loved Jackson Lockewood.

It doesn't seem likely, not when even the idea of giving my heart to someone else feels like a betrayal of who I am and what I know I want.

There is a small creak as the door opens fully, and I look up, half expecting to see Jackson again, conjured as usual from the act of my just thinking about him, but it's only Constance.

"I was on my way downstairs and the door was open," she says, "and I saw it was you in here."

She looks tired, and for the first time, I notice the lines of her face, they're few, but enough to think of how much time has passed.

"Yes, I…" I smile, "I just wanted to see."

She nods and comes towards me, coming to sit beside

me on the bed. "Did I ever tell you that this was my room when I was a girl?"

I shake my head.

She laughs. "Yes, but when I got married, and then Daniel," she looks at me, "my brother got married too and moved into the master suite, I took the suite I use now - It used to be my grandmother's- for whenever I came here with my husband."

She looks a little sad as she talks. I imagine she's thinking about her brother and her husband. They had both died in the plane crash that made her a widow and Jackson and Blythe orphans.

"I didn't know." I say.

She shrugs.

'I'm surprised it's still the same though." I say. "The same as when I left."

"Yes," She pauses, looking as if she's not sure if she should tell me. "I wanted to redecorate it," She says finally, "but Jackson didn't want that."

"Oh." I'm momentarily lost for words. Did he keep the room here as a reminder of what... what we had been, or as a reminder of a mistake he made in the past. I have kept my memories too, made icons of everything he ever gave me, but that's because I loved him with my whole being. What reason could he possibly have for keeping this reminder of my presence in Halcyon?

"He stayed away for so long," Constance continues,

still talking about Jackson. "I thought he was working too hard, trying to prove that he was something more than the latest Lockewood heir." She looks at me, "and he did prove himself you know? Even though there was always a position for him at Lockewood holdings, he preferred to make his own way, going to business school and taking an entry level position in an investment and management firm. That was before he started his own company, made a success out of it, and finally agreed to take over Lockewood holdings." She pauses, "The family has always lived off our investments, but Jackson's built more than just a company managing an investment portfolio. He's taken the risks to build a productive business corporation."

I know that, I want to say. I know all that because we talked about those plans all those years ago, and afterwards, when I left Halcyon, I read everything about him that has ever been published, on the internet, in magazines, from articles on his business methods to his active social life. How pathetic did it make me? That while he worked hard and played hard, I obsessed over him day and night?

"He was always very driven." I say.

She nods, "Yes, driven, determined and disciplined, except when it came to you." After a long pause, she continues. "I didn't see it then. It wasn't until after your accident that I realized you were the reason he'd been home so often in his senior year and that you were also the reason why he never came back after you left. He couldn't bear to come here and be reminded of you in every single room of this house."

Blythe had said almost the same thing, and even Jackson. "Another reason why he hates me." I say with a small laugh.

Constance frowns. "I wouldn't assume that he hates you, dear." She sighs. "When I remember what he was like after you left, I can't imagine why I didn't put it together sooner. If you had seen him then, seven years ago, you wouldn't doubt that he loved you."

"Loved," I reply, "Which means it was in the past, where all these talk and memories should remain." I look squarely at her. "I'm not here to fan the dead embers of a long ago relationship which was always a mistake and should never have happened in the first place. After my job is done, I'll leave, and all our lives can go back to what they were before I came back here."

She sighs. "You're so angry."

"Yes." I cry. "You know what I went through, and I went through it all alone, even more than what you're aware of. So I'm angry, and I have no desire to remember, or relive the past in any way."

Her eyes are glistening as she looks at me. "I can't stop feeling that I failed you in so many ways." She sighs. "I should have told him about the baby."

I close my eyes as her words fill my ears, feeling the familiar pain starting to resurface. When I open my eyes, my fists are clenched so tightly I can feel my nails digging into my palms.

"Don't even mention that, Constance."

"Why not?" She demands, her frown one of confusion, "he deserves to know, he always deserved to know."

"No." I say firmly, trying in vain to shut down the memories and the pain invading my mind. When I left Halcyon, my only thought had been to get as far away as I could from every reminder of Jackson's rejection.

I still remember with clarity how he had made love to me, and then told me coldly that he hated himself for it. The next morning, I left, and found my way to Chace's new apartment in New York, where he was happy for me to stay until the fall semester resumed, or even for longer if I cared to.

Being Chace, he was too involved in his books and research to notice that there was anything wrong with me, and I kept my misery to myself, letting the pain grow inside me like a cancer and eat away at my happiness until I felt like a shadow of who I used to be.

I didn't start feeling ill until school, when I was suddenly too weak to do the things everyone around me was doing, and feeling like I would collapse every time I exerted myself. It wasn't long before I ended up at the school clinic and found out that I was three months pregnant.

Jackson had always been careful, except for that one time in the gazebo, when his anger had made him forget, or stop caring. My baby had been conceived in anger and pain, but it was Jackson's baby, the only thing I had left of him. I knew what my options were, but I never wanted anything as much as I wanted that baby. I was willing to sacrifice school, a career even, for a lifetime to treasure the one thing Jackson had given me that he could never take away.

The next few days I alternated between euphoria at the knowledge that I was going to have a child of my own, to outright dejection at the thought that the father of my child wanted nothing to do with me. It was one of those days that I'd had the accident. I still don't know what happened. One minute I'd been standing on the sidewalk waiting to cross, and the next, a cyclist shoved me out of the way, and that's all I remembered when I woke up in the hospital.

Aunt Constance was there. She was the one who told me I'd lost my baby. The agony was the worst thing I'd ever felt, and the knowledge that it was my fault.

Constance had guessed then that the baby was Jackson's, and when she asked me, I confessed everything, and begged her not to tell anyone about the baby, especially not Jackson.

I left the hospital even more heartbroken than I'd been before, and in the next few months, I spiraled into a debilitating depression, where I spent whole days crying, unable to get out of bed, and not caring if I lived or died.

I missed classes, tests, assignments. I almost dropped out of school, and I would have, if May hadn't blackmailed me out of bed and practically forced me to start living again.

Even though it all happened a long time ago, the misery is always fresh when I think about those days. How I buried myself in schoolwork to try to catch up in my classes, how I masked the pain by keeping myself so busy that I was always too exhausted to think. How I pushed myself, taking classes during the breaks and taking a busy job as a photographer's assistant, so I never had to face the pain I had buried inside me.

"Livvie…" Constance starts.

"Why does he deserve to know anything?" I say bitterly. "I've dealt with it. He's the lucky one who never had to. He didn't lose anything. He didn't end up on a hospital bed, afraid to lose the one thing that still mattered, only to be told it was too late."

"Yes" She agrees, "But if he had known he would never have left your side."

"Only because he would have felt that he had to." I shake my head. "He hated me then and he hates me now. Telling him won't change that. I don't want his pity, so let's not talk about this anymore, please."

She doesn't say anything, but I know from the expression on her face that she'll leave it, for now.

"Blythe said you had been ill." I mention, a little out of concern, but also to change the subject.

"Yes, but I'm better now."

"What was wrong?"

"I had a stroke." She smiles softly as if she still can't believe it herself.

"Oh!" I frown, "I'm so sorry."

She shrugs. "It was stress related. I was unconscious for a while, and for a long time there was a little numbness on my right side, but I'm better now."

"I'm so sorry," I say. "I didn't know."

"You couldn't have." She smiles. "These days I just try to avoid stress. I cut down on all my work, the board meetings, charity work…." She makes a dismissive gesture. "I was never going to work a day in my life, you know. Daniel would have been around to take care of Lockewood Holdings, and Jonathan, my husband, he wasn't the career type. We'd have spent our lives travelling and spending money we never worked for." She sighs, "My whole life changed when they died, suddenly I had two children to take care of, a family legacy to pass to the next generation, and a company that needed me on the board. I could have continued to travel and socialize, but I couldn't bring myself to leave the children. Blythe

195

was only five, and she used to cry for her mom every day. Jackson tried to be strong, but every morning his eyes would be red from crying all night."

Why is she telling me this? I don't want to think of Jackson as a boy, miserable and missing his parents. I don't want to feel this urge to take the man that boy has become in my arms, and comfort him.

"I loved those children Livvie," Constance continues, "I was all they had. Me, each other, and their memories, most of which are rooted in this house." She looks at me. "I spend a lot of time in Rhode island now. Jonathan had a house by the sea. He used to spend holidays there when he was a boy. We spent a lot of time there too, when he was alive."

"Do you like it there?"

She nods. "But that's not why I'm telling you. With me practically living there, and Blythe in the city, this house is unused, and Jackson will give it away."

"He won't"

"He will, if he never gets over the memories keeping him away from here. I know he's thinking about it."

Mrs. Shannon had mentioned the same thing. I can't even imagine Halcyon without Lockewoods in it. For a moment, I allow myself to imagine a new generation of Lockewood children running through the house. Children with Jackson's eyes, Jackson's smile, my children. I shake my head to clear the silly thought. "Have you considered that it might be the expense of maintaining a house as large as this?"

"No," she shakes her head. "The house is maintained by a trust that's separately invested from the family money. If Jackson donates the house to the national trust, the trust will go with the house, so it'll actually cost him more to give it away, in terms of his family legacy, his memories, and money."

"I don't know what you think I can do…"

She sighs. "I just hoped… "She shrugs. 'I'm just a silly old woman looking for happy endings for everyone."

"You're not old." I tell her with a smile. "Maybe it's you who needs to fall in love and have a happy ending. That will make you feel young."

She smiles and gets up. "I'm going downstairs. It's been so nice having a houseful of people again. Will you come down for dinner?"

"Yes."

Later, when she has left me alone, I return to my room and change for dinner. Downstairs, the atmosphere is much the same as it is every other night. Blythe has Nick and Carl wrapped around her little finger, and they alternate between trying to entertain her with juicy city gossip, and listening with rapt attention as she talks. Constance is quiet, listening to the conversations but not taking part. Elaine, no longer sulking at losing all the male attention, has transferred her attention to Jackson. She's sitting on the arm of his chair, looking dainty and gazing adoringly at him, while he smiles at her.

Maybe he has shown her his boat, and from the expression on her face, she must have liked it very much. I shouldn't care, I tell myself, but it's all I can do not to push her off the arm of his chair.

Aside from one searing look when I walk into the room, he mainly ignores my presence, concentrating his efforts on making his devotee laugh over and over again until the sound of her perfectly artful laugh starts to grate on my nerves.

"Constance told me about her stroke," I whisper to Blythe during dinner.

She sighs. "It was scary, at first, but she's much better now."

I nod. "I can imagine," I say, "the scary part. Is she really better?"

"The doctors say she is, and she does look much better than she did during... in the middle of it all. She is taking things a lot easier these days though."

After dinner, Nick has some emails to send and leaves immediately, Blythe goes upstairs with Constance, and I'm left to witness Jackson and Elaine's flirting.

I should leave them. From the pointed looks Elaine is sending my way, I know she wants me to, but some stubbornness makes me stay, a reluctance to leave them alone even though every word they exchange makes me more and more heartsick.

"I can't tell you how much I hate the fact that we'll be leaving soon." Elaine sighs. "I wish we could stay longer."

"Maybe you'll come back." Jackson suggests.

"Oh, I would love that," She breathes in that smoky voice. She sounds like a bitch in heat, I think in disgust, unable to resist the urge to roll my eyes.

"What Olivia?" Jackson doesn't miss the gesture, "Wouldn't you like to come back here?"

I meet his eyes, braving the mocking challenge I find there. "I think I've had enough of small town living for now."

He shrugs.

Elaine tugs on his arm and whispers something to him. I see him get up and go to the side table to pour a glass of amber colored liquid. I can't help staring at him, the perfect body, and the easy and confident way he carried it. Maybe I was wrong to resist, maybe just once I ought to remind my body what it felt like to reach the heights of pleasure his body could give mine.

Embarrassed at my carnal thoughts, I look away and my eyes meet Elaine's. She's staring at me, with a smirk on her face that tells me she knows exactly what I'm thinking. Her eyes are gleaming with a certain satisfaction, which I assume to mean that she sure she already has what she thinks I want.

"Olivia."

"What?" I look up at Jackson, he's half turned from the side table, looking at me questioningly.

"I said would you like a drink?"

"No," I get up. "I'm going to go to bed, I'm suddenly very tired."

His eyebrow quirks, and his eyes say he doesn't believe me.

"Goodnight." Elaine chirps pleasantly.

"Goodnight." I smile at them both, even though inside I have a silly urge to cry. "See you tomorrow."

Upstairs, I wash my face and change out of my dinner clothes. I have no desire to sleep, so I pick up my computer and start to edit a portrait of an actress I was commissioned to do before I came back to Halcyon. I pour all my consciousness into what I'm doing, trying to stop myself from thinking about Jackson and Elaine downstairs, alone, together.

I don't know how much time has passed by the time the door opens, an hour or maybe more. I look up and see Jackson framed in the doorway.

"I thought you said you were tired." He says.

"I thought you would know enough to respect the privacy of a guest in your home," I retort.

"Come on," He laughs. "It's not like you've got anything I haven't seen before." He walks into the room and stops by the bed, where I'm sitting with the computer on my lap. "That looks interesting." He says.

I don't reply, instead I continue adding filters to the image to create a pop art effect.

"Aren't you going to reply?"

"Are you going to start tormenting me again?"

"Is that what I do?" he asks, coming to sit beside me on the bed. I stiffen as his closeness fills my senses. "What if I told you I was the one in torment?" He whispers against my neck, "from having you so close, within reach, from seeing your body respond even without me touching you."

I swallow, fixing my eyes on the image on my screen. "You used to date her didn't you?" I say, changing the subject and taking his attention back to the face on my screen. I read too much about him in the news not to know the names and faces of every single woman with whom he was ever rumored to have an affair.

He chuckles. "When did you start reading gossip magazines Olivia?"

I don't reply.

He considers me silently for a moment. "Why do you want to know? Underneath all your indifference, are you jealous?"

Yes, I am jealous. I hated every single person he was ever photographed with. I hated them almost as much as I loved him. I remove the laptop from my lap and get up, putting some distance between us as I move away from the bed. "I couldn't care less," I retort. "I was just trying to change the subject. Are you jealous of all the men I've been with in the last seven years?"

He's watching me like a hawk. "What if I said I was?" He says, "What if I said that I wanted to make you forget that you were ever with anyone else?"

"I'd say you ought to have your head examined."

He laughs. "I should have my head examined if I can stand to be in the same room with you, and even want it, anticipate it." He gets up and moves towards me, stalking, like a hunter to its prey. "Does it make you feel powerful, to know that you drew me back here, against my better judgment?"

"I don't feel anything when it comes to you," I snap. "Why aren't you somewhere with Elaine, you did spend all evening flirting with her."

"She's not you." He says.

I sigh. "Don't think saying stuff like that will do you any good."

He smiles. "That would mean something if I had any good in mind." His hand catches my wrist and starts to caress the tender skin on the inside. "All I have in mind is the bad things I want to do you."

"Jackson…" I start.

In one swift movement, he pulls me to him, pressing my body flush against his. I can feel the hard muscles of his chest, the thud of his heart against his ribs vibrating against my breasts, I can feel his warmth, and the hard ridge of his arousal pressed against my hips.

I want him. I want him with a desperation I can't seem to control, I want to stroke my hands along his hard length and hear him moan, I want to explore the hard contours of his body with my fingers, my lips, my tongue. I want to lose myself in him, to surrender body and soul.

"What did you do to me?" his voice is harsh. "Why on earth can't I get you out of my mind?"

Through the fog of my arousal, I almost laugh. I should be the one asking him that, I think resignedly.

His hands move up my back, trailing a sweet path up to my shoulders and making me tremble perceptibly. Then he cups my chin and tilts my face so that I'm looking up at him. "Protest all you want," he says, "It won't change the fact that this thing we have between us, it's undeniable."

"Jackson."

"Give in to it. Sweetheart," his voice is soft and tempting. "You know you want to."

I almost give in just then, I almost allow him to take control of my body, to give me the fulfillment I'm is aching for.

His lips are trailing a sweet path along my throat. One hand cups my breast, squeezing softly as he strokes a thumb over a hungry nipple. His other hand moves down through the waistband of my silk pajama shorts to find the warm, pulsing wetness between my legs.

"Olivia." The sound is somewhere between a moan and a sigh as his fingers slip through the wet folds. "Don't say no to me."

I don't want to, not when his hands are doing the most sensual things to my body. My back arches when his finger finds the sweet nub between my legs. When he strokes it I almost lose the power of coherent thought, but my sense of self-preservation rescues me at the last moment. I brace my hands against his shoulders and push away from him, feeling the loss as his fingers slips away, leaving me wanting. "No." I say thickly, "Get out of my room, Jackson. Leave me alone."

"You know better than to think I will," He says, the threat obvious in his soft words. Then he turns and leaves the room, his posture relaxed, as if he hasn't just turned my world upside down.

Chapter Sixteen

I spend the whole night tossing and turning, my body consumed by yearning. Stubbornly I refuse to let my fingers reach for where I'm throbbing uncontrollably and caress myself just as Jackson had done, to close my eyes and imagine him making love to me while I bring myself to a release that would only be a faint shadow of what he could give me, but release nonetheless.

So I toss and turn and try to drown out the sound of Jackson's voice in my head, the memory of his seductive whisper in my ear.

"Give in to me."

Well I won't, even if my body is aching and pulsing with need for him, even if by the time I get out of bed in the early hours of the morning I'm almost crazy with unfulfilled desire.

This cannot continue, I think angrily, as I throw on my clothes. On one hand, I could always let Jackson have his way and give my body what it's obviously craving. But to what end? I can't fool myself into thinking that there's any universe in which I could get Jackson Lockewood out of my system just by sleeping with him. On the other hand, I could always leave. The shoot is practically over, and I've taken all my pictures. The fact that the initial arrangement was to stay in Foster for a week doesn't mean I can't leave a few hours earlier.

After I've pulled on jeans and a light cotton top, I put my hair in a ponytail and make my way downstairs. I'm not a jogger, so I'm not usually out at the first light of dawn. Today, I can see what I've been missing, the patterns in the sky as the first light comes from the east, the stillness in the air, as if everything, the trees, the flowers, and even the grass are waiting for the day to begin. I should have brought my camera I think, as I start to walk down the long drive, then out to the road, but then, my mission this morning has nothing to do with work and taking pictures.

I walk for what seems like a long time, passing only two solitary joggers on the road. When I get to cemetery,

I can't help the feeling of guilt when I think of how long it's been since I was last here. My parents graves are well kept but with none of the personal touches of the graves with fresh flowers and relatives who obviously care enough to visit often.

My eyes scan through the familiar words engraved in the stone, to the phrase at the bottom *'to live in the hearts of those you love is not to die.'* The last time I was here, I dismissed those words, but now I know they're true. I will always see echoes of my mother in the mirror, and when I make an effort to be funny, my humor will always be very much like my dad's. As long as I'm alive, they will always be too.

Over the years, I've sometimes wondered if things would have turned out differently if they hadn't died. Maybe having a mother to talk to would have made me less likely to surrender everything to Jackson. Maybe if I had been living in my own house instead of with Jackson at Halcyon it wouldn't have been so convenient for us to give in to whatever it was that drew us together.

Of course, there's no point in wondering, I realize. It's impossible to change the past. The only thing that matters is never to repeat the same mistakes in the present.

Armed with that thought, I say goodbye to my parents, determined that whatever happened, I wouldn't give Jackson the satisfaction of surrendering myself to him again.

It's already full light when I get back to the house, with the sun high in a beautiful blue sky. There's no one around, so I spend the day reshooting some of the scenes I wasn't totally satisfied with before as well as taking the pictures I know I'll keep for myself. To remind me of the house I loved, where I fell in love.

Even though I move around the house, I don't run into anyone while I work, and I have no idea where Nick is, nor Elaine. By lunchtime, I find Mrs. Shannon in the kitchen.

"I think everyone's feeling sober that you're all leaving tomorrow." She tells me, fixing me a plate on the kitchen table. "Will you be coming back?"

I smile sadly, "I don't think so."

She sighs. "Jackson mentioned that everyone is joining him on the boat after lunch. He said to ask you if you would like to join them."

"I'd rather not."

She smiles. "He said you'd say that?"

I bristle. "What exactly did he say?"

She shakes her head. "Just that you wouldn't want to come. It's always been either sweet or stormy between you two. I suppose right now it's stormy."

"Right now it's nothing," I say with a frown. I don't want to leave Jackson thinking that I'm afraid of him. I know that he'll assume correctly that I'm avoiding him, and he'll know it's because I'm not as indifferent to him as I claim to be. If everyone is going to be on the boat, then what's the harm? He wouldn't try to seduce me in front of his aunt and his sister.

"I think I'll join them," I say, "It's a lovely day to sail anyway."

After I've eaten, I change into shorts and a striped tee shirt, and leave the house through the back, walking through the gardens to the path that leads up to the water front. I'm a little late, so I have a slight hope that they would have gone ahead without me, but that hope is dashed when I see the boat, white and gleaming in the sun, at the end of the wooden dock.

I can't see anybody around. For a second I wonder if I got the message wrong, maybe they decided not to go out after all.

Curiosity makes me climb the stone steps to the dock. I've been on boats before, but I want to see what Jackson's is like. I walk to the end and step unto the boat. As beautiful as it is from afar, it's much more beautiful up close. The deck is spotless and shiny, with cushioned seats and even a coffee table. A door leads to the interior of the boat, where I assume there'll be more luxurious furniture and a well-equipped stateroom. I take a moment to admire the perfection. Everything gleaming with polish and thorough maintenance, but strangely, there's no one on it.

I'm about to turn around when I hear footsteps, I

pause, immediately regretting my decision to get on the boat as Jackson opens the door and steps onto the deck.

Will I ever get over how good he looks? He's wearing a white polo shirt and tan shorts, exposing strong muscled legs and his perfectly built, athletic body. He looks every inch the model image of a glamorous sailor, only a little more real, more flesh and blood and manly than any model could ever hope to accomplish.

I swallow and take a cautious step back. "Where's everybody else?" I ask warily.

He shrugs nonchalantly. "Not here." He says. I watch him with a frown as he loosens the rope tying the boat to the dock, leaving the boat to drift.

"Wait….What…. Aren't we going to wait for them?" I falter. "I thought we were going sailing."

"We are going sailing." He says cryptically.

I watch in horror as the shore, the trees, and the house get farther and farther away. "What are you doing?" I can hear the hysteria creeping into my voice. "Take me back, right now."

He doesn't reply. Instead he comes towards me, looking more menacing with every step, and for a moment I consider jumping overboard and swimming for the shore. But as if he knows what's on my mind, he is at my side in a matter of moments.

"Don't even think about it," He says tightly, his hands around my arms making it impossible for me to move.

"I'm not interested in acting out your abduction fantasy." I snap, injecting as much contempt as I can into my voice.

He laughs softly but doesn't release me. I don't try to struggle, of what use would that be? He's much stronger than I am by any measure. His hands relax around my arms, but he doesn't let go of me. His palms feel as if they're burning my skin, fanning the flames of the desire that's always too close to the surface.

"Let me go, Jackson." I say firmly.

"No." He whispers.

I can feel myself start to tremble. "I can't do this." I whisper, close to tears. I don't want to be near him. It hurts and yet makes me hopeful at the same time. I can't deal with it. "Take me back."

"No." he says again, this time, the hint of tenderness in his voice makes my knees weak.

I look up at him, my eyes questioning, his arms relax at my side. I know he can feel that I'm shaking and I wish desperately that there was a way to disguise my reaction to him.

"I can't take you back." He says softly.

"Why not?" There's a pleading note in my voice, but I don't care. I'm desperate. I'm down to the last remnants of my self-control, and being so close to him, alone on his boat, I know it's only a matter of time before it totally deserts me.

"I can't take you back sweetheart," he whispers, "because I need this." His voice is so seductive, so soft, so full of temptation, and easily capable of destroying all my resolve. His lips graze my neck, and I can't think anymore, "Because I need you," He continues.

"Please don't do this." I plead, I can feel the sting of tears in my eyes, and I don't want to break down in front of him. "Please don't"

"You want this, Olivia?" he urges, his voice almost fervent. "Why do you want to keep denying what you really want?"

Because I love you too much, I want to say. Because I don't want you to make love to me and get me out of your system. Because I know I'll need much more. Because I know I'll never forget you. "Because I don't want you," I say instead.

"No matter what you do," He says, his teeth nipping at my lower lip, "don't lie to me."

He lips cover mine, warm and seductive. He's so tender that my heart squeezes tightly and I can feel tears staining my cheeks. I start to shake violently, trembling as I'm swamped by such a torrent of emotions that I can't control my body any longer. I buckle against him, and he pulls me to his chest, enfolding me in his arms.

There is none of the anger or contempt I've come to expect from him. Instead, he's gentle, making shushing sounds in my ear, and reminding me with his tenderness, of a long ago Jackson, the one I fell in love with. I breathe in the scent of him as I lay my head on his chest, relaxing against his warm strength. I've dreamed of this, I realize, I've wanted this so much.

My tears are staining his shirt. He feels the wetness and lifts my face so he can kiss the tears off my cheeks. "Stop crying." He says tenderly.

My voice catches in my throat as my eyes search his. I can't reconcile this man to the man who has openly shown himself to despise me in the past few days. When he leans down to take my lips, I don't protest. I surrender myself to the hot caress of his lips as they claim mine in a searing kiss.

This time, I don't bother to pretend that this isn't what I want. I kiss him back, hungrily, because I've wanted to do this for years.

He groans and pulls me closer, until my body is molded to his, and I can feel the evidence of his desire for me through his clothes and mine. It makes me want more. It makes me feverish with pent up need.

He lifts me up, easily, as if I weigh nothing, and carries me into the cool interior of the boat, and into the large stateroom. I don't have time to see what it looks like. The decor, the finish, none of it matters. All I can feel is Jackson's lips on mine, his arms around me, his delicious weight on me as he lowers me onto the wide soft bed.

His hands are like fire on my skin. How could I have

done without this for so long? I think feverishly as I pull at the hem of his shirt, anxious to get it over his head and off him.

He laughs softly at my eagerness and helps me pull the offending material over his head, exposing his beautiful chest to me. I want to touch him, to run my hands over that expanse of hard male muscle, but he stops me, going for my t-shirt and pulling it over my head. My bra and shorts follow, leaving me naked except for my panties.

"You're more beautiful than in my memories," he murmurs, looking from my breasts to my face. Impatiently, I reach for his chest, feeling the hard muscle clench under my fingers. Everything about him is better than in my memories, and I can't get enough.

He sighs and lowers his head to take one of my nipples in his mouth, and I lose my senses. My back arches and I moan with pleasure as sensations take over me. I thread my fingers through his hair, and they tighten involuntarily as he licks my nipple, his tongue swirling round the swollen tip. The clenching between my thighs is almost unbearable, and I spread my legs, hungry for him to be deep inside me even as he transfers his attentions to my other nipple, driving me crazy with his lips and tongue.

As if he knows exactly what I need, he moves one hand down through the waist band of my panties and flattens his fingers over the moist center of my arousal, spreading my juices as he caresses me in slow circular motions. I moan helplessly and press against his fingers, enslaved to the pleasure of his ministrations both at my breast and at my core, and in just a few moments, I can't take it anymore. My brain explodes as my body tightens and almost vaults off the bed.

When I catch my breath again, he's trailing kisses down my body, over my stomach and lower. I watch, eyelids heavy, as he hooks his fingers into my panties and pulls them down.

"Take off your clothes," I tell him, my eyes on the hard ridge in his shorts.

His smile is teasing. "If you insist," He replies, dropping a kiss between my legs before getting up to pull the shorts off along with his briefs.

I feast my eyes on the hard length of his arousal, feeling the rush of liquid heat at my core. I move to the edge of the bed and reach for him, my fingers closing around the warm, smooth skin stretched tight over his hardness.

At the touch of my fingers, he closes his eyes "Olivia.' He moans.

I stoke my fingers down from the tip to the base and back again, stroking my thumb over the moisture at the tip and watching as he gets even harder in my hand.

He brushes my fingers away. "I'm sorry Olivia, I've waited too long. I can't wait one more moment.

"Me neither."

Abruptly he sits on the bed and pulls me up so that I'm straddling him, both knees beside his hips on either side, then he positions himself and cups my butt, pulling me closer and sliding slowly inside me.

The pleasure is so intense, my brain shuts down. I'm gripping his shoulder, holding on for support, and feeling as if I'm going to die from the exquisite feeling of being completely and perfectly filled.

His hands move from my butt to my waist, and he lets me fall backwards until I'm half lying and half kneeling, supported by his hands, my breasts exposed to his gaze, then he starts to move in and out of me with an intense, hungry pace.

His hands around my waist are directing our movements, lifting me and bringing me back down to meet the thrust of his hips. The cabin is filled with the sound of my moans as he drives me crazier and crazier with each excruciatingly pleasurable thrust. I reach for his chest, feeling the flexing muscles under skin that's slick with sweat. His eyes are closed, a frown on his brow as he thrusts his hips, sliding sweetly in and out of me. I feel as if I'm going to explode.

He opens his eyes and they are so full of stark helpless arousal, my body clenches, and a sound escapes me that could be anything from a moan to a scream. I shatter around him, feeling his body tense and jerk as he explodes inside me.

He collapses back on the bed, pulling me down until I'm lying over him. He holds me close like that in his arms, both of us breathing deeply. I shudder with residual pleasure when he pulls out of me and moves until we're lying side by side on the bed, facing each other.

"I haven't stopped thinking about this since I saw you get out of that car the first day you came." He murmurs, his eyes holding mine.

I sigh. How long ago that seems now, yet it's only been a few days. What now? I want to ask. Has anything changed? Only I don't need to ask. None of the oceans between us have disappeared. We're still the same people we were an hour ago, only now we've had sex again. Granted it was explosive, soul shattering sex, but that didn't mean that anything had changed.

"Why that look?" Jackson asks, taking my chin in his hands. "Do you regret this?"

I shake my head. "No."

"Good," he says, his grin boyish, happy even as he rolls until he's on top of me, nudging my legs apart with his, "because I'm going to do it again."

He trails a few gentle kisses down my stomach before his fingers find their way between my legs and start to knead me, milking the sensations from the mind-blowing orgasm of just moments earlier. Then his tongue replaces his fingers, finding that little swollen button of pleasure and sucking on it until the world in front of my eyes explodes.

I'm still panting in a sea of sensation when he enters me again. This time his movements are slow, leisurely strokes, igniting me with each thrust. He doesn't take his eyes off me this time, as if he wants to see my every reaction. In moments, my legs are shaking again, and my body clenching around him. I surrender my senses to him, moaning helplessly as I lose control of my body, the pleasure only intensified by his loud groan as he also reaches his climax.

Chapter Seventeen

IT'S dark when we leave the boat. Jackson has steered it back to the dock and tied it up. He carries me in his arms and doesn't put me down even when we reach the ground. I wonder if he's going to carry me all the way back to the house, and he does, his tenderness such a contrast to what I've come to expect that I'd rather die than leave the sense of safety and comfort I'm feeling in his arms.

Thankfully, there's no one in the foyer, and Jackson carries me upstairs, to his bedroom, depositing me on the king sized bed with an endearing gentleness.

"I haven't become an invalid just because we made love all day," I say, watching as he comes to lie beside me.

He laughs. "No, but I want to make up for wearing you out."

"You haven't worn me out." I tell him with a smile.

I watch as an eyebrow goes up. "Really?" He grins. "That's a good thing because I don't intend to leave you alone all night."

Is it possible to condense seven years of missing someone into a few hours of lovemaking, I don't know, but I guess we'll try, and then what? The persistent voice of worry in my head demands, nothing has changed, tomorrow things will go back to the way they were, I'll go back to dealing with my pain, and he'll go back to blaming me for whatever he thinks I did that summer seven years ago.

But for now, I chose not to care.

"I'm going to run you a bath," he announces, "and get you something to eat, then I'm going to make love to you, in the bath, and on the bed. I promise to make you forget everything but my name, and the feel of my hands on you.

"Well, don't make me wait." I tease, "When you make a promise like that you have to get right on it."

He laughs, "I intend to."

Hours later, sated in every way possible, I watch him sleep, marveling at how innocent he looks, like a boy, not like the man who has made me come, over and over again in every way possible. If I didn't know better, I would convince myself that what's happened between us can mean something, but I know better than to expect anything from Jackson. Now that he has spent his anger on making my body his again, there's probably nothing left, except maybe indifference. I sigh.

"What are you thinking?" Even though his eyes are slightly unfocused from sleep, I feel as if he can still read my thoughts and know exactly what's on my mind.

"Nothing," I reply.

"You can tell me."

I search his face. How easy it would be to tell myself that everything has changed, that our physical intimacy has some emotional significance. How easy it would be to share everything I've carried around with me all these years. There's so much he doesn't know, but what would be the point of telling him. I want to get over my pain, not share it, even though I know he's the only one that can make me forget. So I lie.

"I'm not thinking anything."

He pulls me back into the warmth of his arms and goes back to sleep. When I'm sure he's asleep I get up and go back to my room, by the time I have my things together, it's almost morning, and for the second time in a lifetime. I slip away from Halcyon in the early hours of the dawn, my heart heavy, and certain that I'll never come back.

♥ ♥ ♥

The Jackson I'll always remember is the one from my last day at Halcyon, the tender, loving man who made love to me and made me feel as if nothing that happened in the past mattered at all. That's the Jackson I'll carry around in my heart and in my memories, for as long as I live.

"A little more to the right," I tell the tall, beautiful model I'm photographing. Her hair and dress are billowing in the wind from a large fan, and I'm sure she's as tired as I am, but she turns her face, giving me the profile I want.

"Perfect." I call out, taking a quick series of pictures. We're doing one of those rooftop fashion shoots, and it's windy and a little cold. I concentrate on perfecting every shot, shaking off all thoughts of Jackson as I call out instructions and take some more pictures. By the time the shoot is done, I am almost too exhausted to stand.

"That was pretty intense." I look up at the tiny woman with a big mass of orange curls that threaten to bury her face as she offers me a bottle of soda from the snack table. She's Carly French, the fashion director for a small women's magazine who's in charge of the shoot. I've worked with her a couple of times before, and while she's nice, she's also a hopeless gossip.

I shake my head at the soda and watch as she pops it open and drops on a chair beside me. All around us, the workmen are packing up the set while the model changes back into her jeans and t-shirt, turning her back to the rest of us as her only nod to modesty,.

"You look really tired," Carly continues, which I know means I look awful. I feel awful. Most days I want to curl up in bed and cry until I have no tears left. It's only because I've gone down that road before that I'm determined not to make the same mistake twice.

"Just a lot of work," I say, getting up. I start to pack up my equipment. "I'll get these to you." I say gesturing towards my camera.

She shrugs. "So I heard you spent a couple of days upstate at the Lockewood mansion."

New York gossip is one thing that will never cease to surprise me. "I did," I reply wearily.

She looks impressed. "Did you meet Jackson Lockewood? I've never met him, but I've seen him from afar, and he's just sex on legs."

I reply with a shrug.

She gives me an odd look, obviously unimpressed by my lack of enthusiasm. I don't care. I'm not going to talk about Jackson if I can help it.

I leave soon after. On the sidewalk, the city is bustling with people and noise. I hail a cab, and once inside, I allow my mind to drift as I stare at the trees by the sidewalks, their leaves already fading from green into that beautiful shade of autumn brown that means they're soon going to be as dead as I feel inside.

My apartment feels empty, more so now than it did before I went back to Halcyon. Had it always been like this? Did I fool myself into thinking I could be happy, only to have those illusions shattered once I realized that I could only ever have true happiness in Jackson's arms?

It will get better, I tell myself. I've felt this way before. If I could survive the first time, then I will get over Jackson again. But even I know that this time, it's different, the way I feel now is much worse, I'm languishing at the deepest point of loneliness and pain, and I doubt there's anything that can change the way I feel.

I change into pajamas and curl up on the couch with a tub of ice cream, not really paying attention to the string of reality shows that follow one after another on the TV. I don't know how much time passes before my phone rings. It's May.

"How're you?" She asks.

"I'm not sick, or dying May. I'm fine."

"Are you sure? I always feel as if I'm dying when Chace and I have a fight." She sighs. "It's already been two weeks, and I haven't heard you laugh even once. I'm worried. I know how long it took you to get over it the last time."

"The last time I lost a child and almost died." I mumble, annoyed. "Now I'm an adult who had sex with someone she should have avoided. It happens. I'll get over it."

Are you sure you don't want to come over?" May asks. "I'll send a car. You can drink margaritas while I eat ice cream and envy you."

I smile at the image. "No, I'm fine. I swear."

"I still think you shouldn't have left like you did." She says quietly.

How can I argue when sometimes I feel the same way? When I feel as if I should have waited, and taken whatever crumbs Jackson decided to offer me. "I don't want to talk about it," I whisper, hating the sudden catch in my voice and the sting of tears in my eyes.

"Okay, I love you," May says, "See you soon."

I don't remember falling asleep on the couch, but when I wake up, it's dark. I look around, searching for the source of the sound that woke me up, not sure if I heard it in a dream or in reality.

The sound comes again, and through my bleary mind I realize that it's the buzzer.

You're buzzing the wrong apartment, whoever you are. I sink back onto the couch and will the sound to disappear. Maybe they'll call whomever they're here to see. Maybe they'll go away. Maybe they'll leave me alone to suffer my misery in peace.

When I don't hear the buzzing again, I breathe with relief and get up, ready to go to my room and spend the rest of the night in sleep, where at least I can escape from the turmoil of emotions I feel.

The knock on my door almost makes me scream, but It's the words that follow freeze me in place.

"Olivia."

It's Jackson. His voice is unmistakable. Disbelief momentarily robs me of my senses. It can't be.

"Olivia." The knocking starts again, how soon until someone from one of the other apartments decides to see what the disturbance is about? I panic, unsure whether I want to see him. He sounds angry, and I have no desire to face whatever censure I'm sure I'll find in his eyes.

Go away, I mutter to myself, Go away Jackson, please let me get over you.

When the knocking doesn't stop, I know I have no choice but to open the door. I have a fleeting thought about combing my hair, washing the sleep from my face, or maybe changing out of the pajamas I'm wearing to something more presentable, but it only lasts a moment before I realize that it doesn't matter.

I open the door, and my breath catches in my throat. I feel lightheaded as I fill my eyes with the sight of his perfection. His black hair is a little windblown and unruly, but it makes him look even sexier. He's wearing a pale blue shirt rolled up at the sleeves and tucked into a pair of black pants. As usual, he looks good enough to eat.

Chastising myself for staring, I step back to allow him inside, keeping my eyes on his chest, away from the intensity of the glare on his face. He stalks into my apartment, looking beautiful, dangerous, and angry.

"Why did you leave?" He accuses without preamble.

I sigh. Thinking how seven years ago, I would have given anything for him to follow me and ask me this same question, what a huge difference that would have made.

"You shouldn't be here." I say softly.

"Why did you leave?" he repeats. The words are not as angry as before, but sound controlled, as if there is so much more he would like to say, but he's keeping a tight rein on it.

I shrug. "I finished my job."

"I wasn't finished with you."

I fold my arms across my chest and look up at him, the small defensive posture giving me a little boldness, even though I know it's nothing against his strength. "What else do you want with me, Jackson?"

He stares at me silently for a long moment, and then he turns away and paces a few steps. "You left without saying goodbye, not to me, not to Blythe, and not even to Constance. You may well have given her a slap in the face."

I sigh, "I had to go Jackson."

"Why?" The word bursts out of him. "Was it because you couldn't stomach the fact that you let me touch you? That you enjoyed being with me? Do you hate me so much?"

"Don't you?" I whisper. "Don't you hate me that much?"

"No." His voice is gentle, and his expression is a heartbreaking mixture of confusion and sadness, making my heart ache much more than it's doing already. He takes a step towards me and holds out his arms, as if to reach for me, but then he stops and drops them to his side.

"Constance told me everything," He says quietly.

I stare at him in alarm. "Not..."

"Everything," he repeats, his eyes on my face telling me that he knows.

I shake my head wordlessly, turning away from him. "Why?" I say, "Why did she have to tell you? I told her not to."

"She had to." He says gently, "When you left, I think I went a little crazy. I took the boat out and just let it drift, without caring where it took me. You made me happy, Olivia. For the first time in seven years I felt like there was hope, and then you threw it back in my face by leaving."

"I couldn't..."

He shakes his head. "I understand now. I was such a

beast to you all the time, and that last day wasn't enough to change all that. Luckily, Constance found me before I let the boat drift out to open sea." He sighs. "She told me how much of a fool I was being, and then she told me everything you had been through."

I choke as a sob escapes me. As always, the reminder of what I lost, my future with Jackson, the baby we made… it makes me so incredibly sad. This time, he comes to me and draws me into his arms, holding me tightly to his chest. I can't help it. I give in to the tears.

"I didn't know." I say through my sobs, "not at first." How many times have I imagined of telling him this? How many times have I imagined the condemnation in his eyes? Now the only thing I can see is tenderness, and it kills me inside.

"When I found out, I was too scared to tell you. I didn't know what you would say." I look up at him, my eyes imploring. "I wasn't trying to hurt myself." I tell him earnestly, the same thing I'd said to Constance at the hospital all those years ago, when she'd thought I tried to kill my baby and myself. "I didn't step into the road on purpose." I say desperately, "There was a bike messenger and I was right in front of him…"

"Shhh." Jackson whispers, drawing me closer, "I know it wasn't your fault." His hands are rubbing my back, soothing and tender. "God I'm so sorry," He says, "I should have been there."

I sigh. "Constance was at the hospital when I woke up." I tell him. "She was the one who told me I'd lost the baby. She guessed then that it was yours, but I made her promise never to tell you. I didn't want you to hate me any more than you already did."

He hugs me tighter, until my tears are wet pools on his shirt and my nose is filled with the scent of him. "I never hated you Olivia," He tells me, "I always loved you, always."

"But you were so angry."

"Yes I was." He admits, "That night seven years ago, I was so angry I wanted to kill Carter, and I would have, if I had been the one to walk in on him touching you. When I left, I wanted to hurt someone, to howl at the moon, anything. I couldn't stand to be around all those people at the party. So I left, and drove as far as I could.

"But you came back."

"Yeah, after falling sleep in my car, by the time I got back home, I was still so angry, I didn't want to see anyone, you, Constance, Blythe... so I went to the gazebo," He pauses, "and then you came."

I remember how miserable I had been that day, how I had also been trying to avoid him, and then I had walked straight to where he was.

"I took my anger out on you because I wanted to punish you for making me feel so powerless. Olivia, because that's what you did, you made me feel like a fool for all the dreams I had been building about our future, for thinking that you loved me. When I left you there, I told myself that if I meant nothing to you, if being with me was just a game to you, a way to pass the time until Carter or someone else came around, then I didn't care. I could go to school and date anyone I wanted, so I tried to do that, but I had to come back, to see you."

"But... When you came, you acted like you couldn't stand the sight of me." The memory fills me with renewed pain.

"And yet I couldn't keep my hands off you. As soon as I saw you, I knew everything I'd been telling myself was a lie. I didn't want to move on, I wanted you, and I wanted you to want only me." He laughs softly, "I was crazy about you, little more than a child, and I was so crazy I couldn't help myself."

"Then you left... The next day, and I tortured myself with the thought that I'd driven you away. After you called Constance and told her you were going to stay with a friend in New York, she told me that it had all been Lindsay. I think she thought you left because you hadn't forgiven her. But I knew it was me, and I couldn't forgive myself. I imagined how much you must have hated me for not even asking you what happened and I hated myself so much. I couldn't believe that I had been so blinded by my jealousy, I didn't even give you a chance. I left you all alone, when I should have stood by you."

"I didn't hate you." I deny. "All I wanted was for you to let me tell you the truth."

"I didn't know that," he says earnestly, "All I could think was how despicable I was, how I didn't deserve you." He shakes his head, "By then you were living with Chace, and I tortured myself with the thought of him picking up the pieces I had so carelessly broken."

I shake my head. "But Chace and I were just friends."

"I know that now, but then, I convinced myself of a lot of things, that you had moved on, that you had gotten over me, that you were happy, and I hated you for it. I was a mess. I convinced myself to hate you, it was much better than loving you when you weren't mine. If I had known what you were going through… "

"It doesn't matter now," I smile through my tears. "It was such a long time ago,"

"Yes... but not a day goes by that I haven't thought about everything that happened then. What I knew of it, or what I thought I knew. When I saw you in that restaurant three years ago, I almost went crazy. As far as I was concerned, it was further proof that you had moved on, when I was still flailing around, trying to forget." He sighs, "You've always been a part of me Olivia, no matter how hard I tried to fight it, or deny it."

"Like a brand on my heart." I tell him.

He chuckles, "Exactly. You branded yourself deep inside my heart, no matter how hard I tried to get your mark out, it never worked. I think on some level. I didn't want it to.

I know what he means. "Me too."

"I love you." The words are simple and plain, and I realize that it's the first time he has ever said them to me.

I giggle, a bubble of happiness, bursting out of me. "I love you too Jackson Lockewood, I have since I first saw you.

He kisses me. "I love you," He says again, later. "I want to make it up to you Olivia. Everything. Will you let me?"

I'll let him do whatever he wants. "What did you have in mind?"

"How about the rest of my life?" he asks, "Every day to show that you'll never be alone as long as I'm alive?"

Is he asking what I think he's asking? "Jackson…" I start hesitantly.

He drops down on one knee before I have a chance to ask my question. "I got this on my way here because I was determined that no matter what happened, I wouldn't let you leave me again." He pauses, "You don't have to say yes right now."

"Yes." I interrupt, throwing my arms around his neck, not caring is I seem too eager… too happy, because that's exactly what I am. "Yes, Jackson, I'll marry you."

He expels a breath, his face breaking into a happy smile. He gets up, lifting me up along with him, and when he kisses me, I give myself up to him, because I've always... always belonged to him, only to him.

The End

About Serena Grey

Serena is obsessed with books. She reads everything, from history, to the classics, to novels and even comic books. (Go Walking Dead☺). She started writing because the many stories in her head wouldn't leave her in peace otherwise. Even though she loves all kinds of fiction, she has a soft spot for love and romance, and that flush of pleasure that can only be found at the end of a beautiful love story.

When she's not reading and writing, she enjoys cocktails, coffee, numerous TV shows, has never gotten over her crush on Leonardo DiCaprio, and if she had to choose between a good book and a tub of ice-cream, she'd take both and make a run for it.

Connect with Serena

Facebook: www.facebook.com/authorserenagrey

Twitter: @s_greyauthor

Goodreads: www.goodreads.com/serenagrey

Author Website: www.serenagrey.com

Books by Serena Grey

A Dangerous Man Series
Awakening: A Dangerous Man #1
Rebellion: A Dangerous Man #2
Claim: A Dangerous Man #3
Surrender: A Dangerous Man #4

Find at www.serenagrey.com/a-dangerous-man-series/

From The Author

Thank you all so much for taking the time to read this book. I hope you all enjoyed it. Writing has always been my dream, and I'm eternally grateful to the wonderful readers who have made that dream a reality.

Reviews are awesome! So if you'd like to tell me what you think about this book, don't hesitate to send me a shout out on Twitter or Facebook. You can also leave a review at the purchase site, on Goodreads, on your blog, or anywhere else you like.

You can always reach me at serenagreyauthor@gmail.com, as well as on my Facebook page or via Twitter.

Serena Grey